MARCUS

by

Valerie M. Walland

To Margaret with love, Valerie (VMW)
July 2002

Silverdale Books

Marcus

ISBN 0-9539567-1-7

Published by Silverdale Books
42 West Malvern Road
Malvern
WR14 4NA

Design & production co-ordinated by:
The Better Book Company Ltd
Hampshire PO9 2XH
+44[0]2392 481160

Printed in England.

Cover design by Dudley Brook

Distant growls of growing discontent
Echo from a horizon
Darkened by gathering forces
Of black protesting clouds.

Storm from "Seascape" – Nick Balmforth 1993

AUTHOR'S NOTE

This is a work of fiction set against the background of real events. Some characters therefore did once walk the Earth. I apologize if any action or discourse attributed to them offends their shades.

VMW

Other work by the Author:
EVER WHIRLING WHEELS –
Published by Silverdale Books.

CHAPTER ONE

Marcus was beginning to lose his temper. He had always thought his mother too lenient with the slave.

"A slave is a slave, Mother. They do as they are told, they know their place and, if they don't give satisfaction, they are whipped. Look what she has done to my tunic!"

He held out the torn garment for her inspection.

"Please don't shout, Marcus. People in the street will hear."

"Mother, we are five storeys up! That's another thing, why can't we move from this place? It's falling apart. I noticed a new crack in the wall this morning. Surely we can afford to live somewhere better?"

"I know you miss our old house, Marcus, but what else could I do? There was no money to rebuild the house after the fire and you were only a child. We were lucky that Gnaeus Maius let us have this apartment at such a low rent."

Marcus could still remember the house which had seemed huge to his childish mind. The garden, although small, was his favourite place. It had a pool with fountains and fish. His mother had been always smiling and happy in those days and content to be with him in the garden. Now she hardly ever smiled and spent all her days talking to Murdia about the past which seemed more real to her than the present. He remembered the fire, how frightened he was. How the slaves ran away in panic only Murdia staying to help them escape. They had lost everything they owned. After walking the streets for what seemed like hours they had met a man who brought them to this cramped, crumbling apartment where they now lived.

Knowing it would do no good Marcus still had to ask what he had asked many times before.

"Why not go to your family? It's 18 years since you left the Vestals and you have never, in all that time, asked your family for help."

"We have gone over this before, Marcus. Do please try to understand. I don't want anything to do with my family. I shall never forget the day…"

"Here we go!" Marcus sighed.

"…I was taken to the Vestal's House. When my father told me where I was going I cried and begged him to take my sister instead. He was extremely angry and told me I should be very honoured to be one of the six Vestal Virgins to tend the sacred fire. I was only six years old, Marcus."

Marcus could not understand why she was so bitter. True, she had been forced to sever all ties with her entire family plus all hope of a normal family life, at least until she had completed her 30 years, but she must have become reconciled to her situation eventually. After all, the Vestals enjoyed more freedom than any other women and most men, being only answerable to the Chief Priest. When the Vestal Virgins walked the streets of Rome wearing their distinctive clothes, their hair tied with special hairbands, their lictors walking in front carrying the fasces, the bundle of rods which were the symbol of office, they drew respect from everyone without exception. Many times he had heard the description of the luxurious house in which they lived; the 50ft room with its book buckets containing the wills deposited with the Vestals for safe keeping by Rome's citizens; the plaster flowers, the lavishly painted ceilings picked out in gilt; the wall paintings; the statues. Marcus felt that he knew every inch of the house – not that, as a male he would be allowed to set foot past the public reception room. Their duties were light, they had servants at their beck and call day and night and all they had to do was guard the sacred flame, perform certain rituals connected with the goddess and remain chaste.

"Yes, I know, Mother. You've told me a hundred times before. But later, when you grew older, surely you enjoyed all the dinner parties, the Rites, the best seats at the Games, the freedom?"

Julia continued as if he had not spoken.

"As I walked through that door, I made up my mind that I would leave as soon as I could and I would *never* speak to any of my family again."

Marcus sighed in exasperation. You would think that, since she seemed to hate it so much she would be only too pleased to forget the life as soon as she left but she talked about it constantly. He suspected that she had not realized what a luxurious and easy life she had until she no longer had it. Thinking to divert her he asked

"Tell me again about the day you met the condemned man."

He knew this was her favourite story.

"I have told you many times, Marcus but, since you ask, I'll tell you again."

He had known she would not be able to resist it.

"I was on an errand for the Chief Vestal, I forget what it was, anyway, as I walked down the street I saw, coming towards me, a man in chains escorted by soldiers. As soon as he saw me his face lit up. He knew that his life had been spared. I shall never forget it."

"How fortunate for him to meet you, Madam." Murdia said.

Trust Murdia to put in her denarius worth, Marcus thought. As he watched them talking animatedly together he wondered where the slave had originated. Of course he knew what Julia had told him – she had bought Murdia as soon as she realized she was pregnant but she had never told him any of the slave's history. He studied the slave, trying to work out where her native home might be. Murdia was large and short with a face that could be any age and very black hair. She was certainly older than his mother. She could be from anywhere. He had to admit that she was devoted to her mistress. Becoming aware of his scrutiny she asked

"Anything wrong, Marcus?"

That was another thing. She always used the familiar form of address. As the only male in the household, by all the rules of Roman Society, he was entitled to be called 'Master'. He had pointed this out several times but she always laughed and said that when he had done something to earn the appellation she would comply with his request.

"No." He replied with a scowl.

Turning back to Julia, Murdia fussed with the chair cushions.

"There, Madam, now you will be more comfortable."

"Thank you, Murdia. What would I do without you?" Julia murmured with a smile.

It had always been his mother and Murdia, talking together in low tones, stopping when they thought he was listening. He felt, not for the first time, excluded and unwanted. There was something he had long wanted to ask.

"Mother, when I was born why didn't you expose me?"

Julia was startled and paused for a long time before replying

"Had you been a girl of course I would have done so but, as Murdia pointed out at the time, a boy would keep me in my old age. You must find yourself a Patron, Marcus. I've told you before."

He knew that he needed a Patron and it was not for the want of trying. He had spent days in the reception rooms of some of the most influential men in Rome hoping to get a chance to see the great man, only to be told by a smug Greek secretary.

"My Master regrets he cannot see you today. Perhaps tomorrow?"

But things were no different the next day or the day after. If he only had an influential family to back him he was sure he could find a patron. If Julia would only tell him the family name he could contact them. Once they acknowledged his existence they would be duty bound to do something for him. His Grandfather must have been a Senator at least otherwise his mother would never have been accepted as a Vestal Virgin.

"Perhaps Marcus could become a private tutor, Mistress." Murdia suggested.

"No, Murdia, Marcus can do better than that. He must find a Patron and he'll not get far until he does."

"Mother, it would all be so much easier if you would only contact your family."

The discussion had come full circle, as usual.

"I have told you, no, Marcus."

Julia was, as usual, firm in her refusal.

"At least tell me who my father was. I'll go and see him and demand he take care of us."

As usual, at the mention of his father, Julia became very agitated and, removing her hand from his arm put it to her head saying wearily.

"You know the answer to that, Marcus. I have no idea who your father was only that he was a Military Tribune".

"Which Legion?"

"I have no idea."

"Surely he told you his name?"

"He said his name was Marcus. Just Marcus. I named you after him. I have told you so many times. I had left the House of the Vestals after visiting the Chief Vestal and was on my way back to the house I had just bought, it was very dark and as I crossed the street I tripped and would have fallen into the road had a man not caught me. He insisted on escorting me to my house, so I asked him in."

"You had no idea at the time who this man was?"

"No, I had never seen him before."

Marcus wondered, not for the first time, how much of this story was true. Julia had been a Vestal after all. Vestals were trained to be extremely circumspect. He could not imagine that she would throw off thirty years of training so easily. She must have known him. He had to know who he was.

"What about your slaves? They might have known who he was. Slaves know everything."

"No, I'm sure they did not."

"Murdia?"

"How could she – she didn't come until afterwards. You are always asking me these questions although you know it gives me a headache. I think you are being very unkind."

She began to sob which was the way it always ended.

"Now look what you've done. Have you no thought for your poor mother? Come mistress, come to bed." Murdia led Julia away.

Marcus picked up the chair cushion and threw it at the wall. It really was too much. Every time he began to question her closely she resorted to tears and every time Murdia took her off to bed. He was sure the slave knew more than she admitted. Julia and Murdia were more intimate than was usual with a mistress and slave. Why had Murdia not been sold along with the other slaves unless she knew something that Julia wanted kept hidden? Murdia had always been there, in the background, always watching and listening. He knew they could barely afford to keep themselves let alone a slave. He must find a career but how could he be expected to rise in the world if he didn't have any help from his father? It was a father's duty to provide for his son. He was certain that Julia knew exactly who his father was but for some reason, she was afraid to name him. He would probably never get at the truth. Feeling frustrated and angry he ran downstairs to the street. He would go for a long walk. He hoped that, by the time he got back, Julia would be ready to tell him the truth although he doubted it.

CHAPTER TWO

It was a hot Spring afternoon and Rome seemed to be more crowded than ever. Where did they all come from? The Sacra Via was full of sweating slaves carrying litters, men with loads, women with whining children who got underfoot. A column of soldiers headed by a red-faced centurion came marching straight down the street holding up wagons and causing even more congestion. Marcus's temper was not improved by being nearly hit in the face with a plank of wood being carried by a slave. Then he had to dodge a litter carried by huge slaves, the escorts casually knocking people out of its way. Finding himself outside the Sacra Via Inn he checked his money pouch to see if he had any of the money left that Julia had given him to pay into the Funeral Club. To his relief he had more than enough to pay for a glass of Sabine wine. Looking round the room he spotted his friend Fabrius Decimus. As he joined him Fabius asked

"I know that look, another row at home?"

"The same old thing. If only I knew who my family were – could be related to Caesar for all I know."

Marcus grumbled.

"Funny you should say that. Sometimes in a certain light I have thought..."

"What?"

"Nothing. Oh well, you could always come with me when I join the Army."

Marcus had forgotten that Fabius was thinking of an Army career. He was a good friend who was always ready to lend money when needed.

"I shall miss you, Fabius."

"Come with me then. We can enjoy ourselves. Plenty of travel. Bound to be plenty of girls. Good pay, good food. I can't wait!"

"I'll think about it."

"Well don't take too long. I shall be off soon. Now, I must go."

After Fabius left Marcus sat on for a while longer thinking of his future. He was young and now was the time to lay the foundations of his future career. He considered Fabius's suggestion of the Army but dismissed it. The only way he could enter the Army was as an ordinary soldier but he did not fancy spending years working his way up to the rank of Centurion, not to mention the possibility of being killed before he got that far. If only he had been born into a normal family! If only she had never left the Vestals! Most Vestals never left the order even when their 30 years were finished, let alone had illegitimate babies! If he only knew the family name he could do anything – become a Senator perhaps. A sudden thought struck him like one of Jupiter's lightning bolts. Of course! The gods must have a special destiny for him! Excited, he leapt up and left the Inn.

He walked for some time, taking no notice of his surroundings until he found himself going through the Arch of A. Fabius Allobrogicus and up the steep Clivus Sacer. He stopped to admire one of elegant houses. For all he knew his Mother's family lived in that spacious house while he existed in a cramped two-bedroomed apartment at the top of a building where he roasted in summer and froze in winter, not to mention all the stairs he had to go up and down every day. If the gods did have a special destiny for him he wished they would show him what it was. He wondered who lived there. The person in that litter perhaps which, carried by six slaves, was making its way down the road. Probably some rich Senator's wife back from spending her husband's money. As the litter passed him he tried to see inside but the curtains were closed. Ignoring the knocks and curses from the crowd flowing up and down the street, he turned to see where the litter was heading. Would it stop at one of the houses or would it continue through the Arch, he idly speculated.

Suddenly, above the noise of the street, he heard shouting. Turning round, he saw a wagon, clearly out of control, careering back down the hill dragging the horses with it. The panic-stricken driver leapt from the wagon, landed in the road, and lay still. Swaying violently, the wagon careered across the road, shedding its load of marble slabs and burying a number of people. Screaming pedestrians scattered in all directions. The slaves carrying the litter dropped it and ran. It was inevitable that the wagon would topple on to the abandoned litter.

Afterwards Marcus was horrified at his actions, now he did not stop to think but ran to the litter where, after pulling back the curtains, he just had time to register that the occupant was female, beautiful, and unconscious, before plucking her from the litter and leaping onto the pavement, seconds before the wagon toppled over reducing the expensive litter to matchwood.

A white-faced Porter came running from one of the houses.

"Is the Mistress dead?"

"No, but she is unconscious. We must get her into the house. She needs attention."

"I'll get the Chief Household Slave."

The Porter ran back into the house calling "Lucius! Lucius!"

A slave came hurrying out, ordering the Porter back to his Box by the door.

"Bring the Mistress through here, Master".

Marcus followed Lucius through the atrium to one of the reception rooms where he laid the woman down on a couch. Several slaves crowded in the doorway.

"Fetch the Mistress's slave and go about your business" Lucius ordered.

The slaves fled.

While they waited Marcus had time to study the woman. Her green mantle had slipped from her shoulder to reveal an expensive emerald and gold necklace so, she was not only young and beautiful but, more importantly – rich.

A female slave appeared and began waving a small bottle beneath her Mistress's nose who coughed and pushed the woman's arm away. Both slaves were concentrating on their Mistress which gave Marcus a chance to note the expensive furniture, the wall paintings, the statues. Plenty of money here. Perhaps some would come his way.

"Get your Master," he ordered.

"No, Lucius." The rescued woman opened her eyes and asked, faintly.

"What happened?"

"A wagon ran down the hill out of control. When your litter slaves realized it was going to fall on to the litter they dropped it and ran away. Fortunately *I* was walking down the hill at the time, so I rescued you."

Marcus was pleased that, without boasting, he had managed to convey the fact that she should be grateful to him and him alone.

"Thank you —?"

She looked at Marcus enquiringly.

"Marcus Rutilius".

"I am Annia. I am in your debt, Rutilius, you saved my life."

Marcus was hoping she would mention some monetary reward instead she ordered.

"Find the litter slaves and have them flogged, Lucius."

"Yes, Mistress."

She turned back to Marcus

"Excuse me, I must rest. Lucius will show you out."

Marcus was not pleased at being dismissed in so summary a fashion. He had saved her life after all!

Lucius indicated the way out. But Marcus was not going to let slip the chance of some reward. Accordingly, when they arrived at the Porter's Box he turned to the slave and said, in his most aristocratic manner.

"Lucius, I expect your Master will want to thank me in person. A note to the Inn on the Via Lata will find me."

No need to mention that he lived in the Subura, the poorest district of Rome.

Lucius bowed but did not reply.

Finding his way to a tavern he had a modest dinner of bread, sardines and lettuce leaves washed down with a jug of watered wine, after which he felt more cheerful. No need to rush back to the apartment. He decided to call in at his favourite tavern where he knew he would find some of his friends. They were all there and he got into a dice game during which he lost the rest of the Burial Club money. He had to win it back – the money was due to be paid at the Club Dinner which was only a few days away. If he didn't go to the dinner someone was bound to tell Julia then there would be tears, recriminations and Murdia would flay him with her tongue.

To his dismay, he had not recouped the money by the time the Tavern closed at sunset. Disgruntled, he made his slow way home. By the time he turned into the road where the apartment block that he called home was situated it was dark. He was tired. All he wanted to do was to go to bed. He knew that his mother would be sitting up waiting for him as usual. There seemed to be a great many people about. Something must be going on. He quickened his pace then stopped, stunned – the five storey block that he had left so angrily that morning, was a pile of rubble in which men dug by the light of torches.

Marcus was horrified. His best toga had gone! What would he do now? He only had the clothes he stood up in, hardly any money and nowhere to sleep tonight. As he stood at the back of the crowd he heard two men in front of him discussing the tragedy.

"Do you know how many were killed?" one asked

"They've brought out several bodies. As it happened when most people were having their evening meal. I expect there will be more, although if they were on the top floor there is not much chance of finding enough to identify them."

"It's time the Senate did something about these landlords. They take the rents and never do anything to keep the properties standing."

"I expect most of the Senate *are* the landlords!"

Laughing, the men moved away.

Seeing one of the neighbours from across the street looking in his direction Marcus moved back into the shadows. He had just realized that he was, officially at least, dead. Dead men could not be asked to pay for funeral rites or settle their debts and neither did they have to go into mourning and isolation for eight months. He was free to go anywhere he liked; do whatever he wanted.There was not one single person in the entire known world who had any claim upon him. But he would have to get out of Rome. In the meantime he needed somewhere to stay away from his usual haunts and that would need money.

Of course! Annia! She lived in the better part of Rome, somewhere where no one would look for him even if they had a suspicion that he was still alive. As for money, he *had* saved her life, that must be worth enough money to get him on a ship out of Rome. He was sure her husband would want to show his gratitude. He would go there at once.

Most of the narrow streets were dark, the moon covered by cloud affording only a fitful illumination. He made slow progress as he had to watch where he was walking so that he did not wrench an ankle in one of the many potholes whilst, at the same time he was kept busy dodging the contents of basins thrown from top floor windows. Not many lone travellers were abroad and those he did see scuttled past, anxious to get home as soon as possible. Rome was a dangerous place at night. Several litters passed him escorted by large slaves armed with thick staves and blazing torches.

He had just passed the Sacra Via Baths and was thanking Jupiter Optimus Maximus that he had not run into trouble, when he saw a group of rowdy young men and their slaves plainly on the rampage. He quickened his pace as he heard them coming. He did not have far to go now so he turned left and took the narrow Via Nova in the hope of avoiding them. He would have a much longer walk but it would be worth it.

As he entered the alley he saw a female figure he recognized coming towards him. He groaned – of all people it had to be Terentia! He owed the prostitute two Sesterce and it was one of the many debts he hoped he had written off by "dying". He had only got away from her last time by promising to pay her the next time he saw her. He could not risk her recognizing him, it would be a disaster as he knew she would not be happy until she had been paid down to the last denarius. Unfortunately, as he knew only too well, she had a very loud voice which she would undoubtedly use to rouse the whole of Rome thereby destroying any chance he had of remaining incognito.

He tried desperately to think of a way out. He could tell her that he was a shade – a ghost of himself. No, that would not do, it was too risky – she was bound to scream. He would have to retreat. Perhaps the youths would not see him. He turned and walked back to the junction only to come face to face with a young man wearing a crumpled garland and a wine-stained toga.

"Stop, you!"

Marcus, being no hero did as he was ordered.

"Who are you, then?"

"Rutilius."

"Well, *Rutilius*, let's have your money."

"I don't have any money."

"No money! And roaming round Rome at night! I don't think you're telling the truth, Rutilius. We will have to search for it, won't we!"

Before Marcus could do anything to defend himself his cloak was torn from his shoulders and he was bundled onto it by the slaves who, holding the edges raised him, struggling, into the air where he was tossed like a salad, to cries of:

"Where is the money? It must be on him somewhere. Toss him higher."

"I *have* no money!" Marcus gasped.

The slaves tossed him until, their masters catching sight of a more promising victim, they were ordered to let him go and he was dropped unceremoniously onto the cobblestones where he lay, groaning. Not until he was sure they had left did he stagger to his feet, feeling dizzy. He must be more careful, he doubted he could survive another such encounter.

His tunic was torn and his cloak had disappeared. Blood began to run down his face and upon investigation he discovered a cut on his forehead. He ached from head to foot and did not want to think what he would feel like in the morning. Twice he had to take refuge in doorways from gangs of youths. When he eventually got to the Clivus Sacer it took him a long time to wake the Porter who, as soon as he recognised him, sent for the Chief Household Slave. Just as Lucius arrived Marcus, feeling faint, slid down onto the black and white tessellated floor. Lucius, alarmed, sent the Porter for help which arrived in the shape of two burly male slaves who hauled him to his feet and held him upright.

"I must see your Master." Marcus gasped.

"Wait here, Master."

The slave was away a long time and Marcus was thankful for the support of the two slaves. While he waited he assessed the damage so far as he was able. His tunic was badly ripped and, as well as the cut to his head, he had various scratches and bruises which were beginning to go purple. He had lost a sandal and the foot was bleeding where he had been walking on the cobblestones. Altogether he did not look very heroic.

Eventually Lucius returned and, dismissing the slaves, told him

"The Senator will see you. Follow me."

He led Marcus to a richly furnished triclinium where Annia was lying on a dining couch eating peaches from a silver dish held by a slave. Another slave held a basin and cloth. Lying next to her was the Senator, a stern-faced man with close-cropped white hair, deep-set eyes and a patrician air.

As Marcus entered the room Annia looked up with a small, affected scream.

"Oh! you poor thing. What has happened to you? Sextus Caius Quintilius, this is the brave young man who saved my life when your wretched litter slaves ran away. Have they been caught yet, Lucius."

"No, Mistress."

The Senator's close scrutiny made Marcus very conscious of his disreputable appearance.

"Your name?"

"Marcus Adiutor."

Marcus remembered, just in time, that he was dead. He hoped that Annia would not remember his name from the morning. He doubted whether she would.

"Have you dined?" Sextus enquired.

"No."

Marcus made it a policy never to refuse a free meal.

"Lucius."

"Master?"

"Take our guest, get his wounds attended to and find him a tunic." He turned to Marcus "We will talk when you return."

After an army of slaves had bathed him in the well appointed bath suite, put soothing unguents on his wounds and provided him with clean clothes Marcus felt almost his old self. As he entered the triclinium Sextus looked up and gave a start. Marcus was not surprised, he knew he was handsome. Sextus indicated a place on the opposite couch.

"Now, tell me what happened."

Increasing the number of attackers to twenty youths plus their slaves, Marcus casually added that he had also been robbed of quite a considerable sum of money.

"When I went back to the building where I had a rented apartment I found it had collapsed taking everything I own with it."

"Oh! How awful. What will you do now?" Annia fluttered.

Marcus shrugged.

"I don't know. I shall have to find somewhere I suppose."

Sextus looking thoughtful asked, "Some wine?"

Marcus nodded.

"What would you like?" Marcus automatically replied.

"Sabine, please."

"Oh, I think we can do better than that."

The Senator motioned to a slave.

"Our guest will have the Falernian."

Marcus had never tasted Falernian, such rare and expensive wines did not flow in his direction. He found it was good and determined then and there that, somehow, some day, he would be in a position to drink it whenever he wanted without worrying about the cost.

The slaves brought him fish with garum sauce, then Numidian chicken followed by a dish of fruit served on plain silver dishes. This was a far cry from the cabbage, leek soup and sheep lips served on clay dishes he got at home.

When there was nothing left to eat Marcus sighed deeply and allowed a slave to wash his hands. Once the mess had been cleared away and he could pay attention to his surroundings he realized that no one had spoken for some time and that the Senator was regarding him thoughtfully.

"So, you are homeless, Adiutor. Do you have anywhere to stay? Any friends or relations who could take you in?

"I live alone. My mother died two years ago."

"And your father?"

"My father, a Military Tribune, was killed in Gaul when I was a baby. I never knew him."

That took care of that.

"But you have a Patron I presume?"

"Not at the moment."

Sextus nodded.

"Adiutor – I can't recall a Tribune of that name in Gaul. Which Legion?"

Marcus plucked one from the air.

"The Xth."

"The Xth! Caesar's favourite Legion." Sextus sounded thoughtful. "Well, no matter, I have an idea which could help us both. I have a villa at Baeae that Annia has been pestering me to take her to before the heat in Rome becomes intolerable. Unfortunately, I am unable to leave Rome for some time and, since it is still early in the season and Baeae is quite empty at the moment, I was not prepared to let her travel alone with only the slaves for protection. However, it would solve the problem if you went with her."

"I will be happy to do so, Senator".

Marcus could not believe his luck – he could get away from Rome and at someone else's expense!

"Good, also it will give you time to decide what you are going to do and, in the meantime, you can stay here."

Pouting prettily Annia cried.

"Oh, Sextus! What a pity you can't come too! Are you sure you must stay in Rome?"

"I am afraid so, but you will have Adiutor for company and the time will soon pass. Take Lucius and any other slaves you think you may need."

"It will not be the same without you, Sextus but I suppose there is no help for it. You will come as soon as you can, won't you?"

"I shall be there before you know it, Annia, I promise you. Lucius!"

"Yes, Master?"

"Prepare a room for our guest."

"Yes, Master."

Turning back to Marcus Sextus said

"You will need some money for your immediate expenses, Adiutor. You can pay me back later."

So saying, Sextus rose and left the room returning a short time later with a money bag which he handed to Marcus.

As Marcus put the bag away in his money pouch Annia asked.

"You're not going to spend the evening in your study again, Sextus, are you?"

"I am afraid so. I have a great deal of work to do before the Senate meets tomorrow. I will see you in the morning."

Once they were alone, Annia seemed inclined to chat but Marcus, pleading pain and fatigue, said he was going to bed. Calling for Lucius Annia ordered the slave to show Marcus to his sleeping cubicle.

Picking up a lamp Lucius led the way to an adequately but not luxuriously furnished sleeping cubicle. As he lit the tall lamp by the clothes cupboard Lucius asked

"Is there anything else, Master?"

"No, you may go."

The slave bowed and left the room.

Marcus was pleasantly surprised to find the bed, mattress and pillows very comfortable. A luxury after the thin mattress he was used to. He had a thought and checked – yes, there was even a chamberpot! He was not used to such luxury.

He sighed with contentment. Who would have thought that he would end the day motherless, homeless and with more money than he had seen in a long time. He placed the money bag under his pillow, extinguished his lamp, climbed into bed and was soon sound asleep.

CHAPTER THREE

The day after his arrival, and despite feeling as if every muscle had been massaged by the huge Numidian slave at the Surburan Baths, Marcus decided to replace his wardrobe so asked and obtained, much to Annia's annoyance, permission from Sextus to use the litter thus enabling him to travel in a closed litter to the Porticus Maguiritaria without worrying about anyone he knew seeing him. Once there he went swiftly into the most prestigious shop and spent a happy morning choosing clothes, eventually returning to the Clivus Sacer confident that he could dress appropriately for any occasion. But, to his disappointment, Sextus and Annia were the only people who saw him in his new clothes as, despite Annia's pleas, Sextus declined either to take advantage of the numerous dinner invitations he received or to entertain at home, pleading pressure of work. Marcus was, therefore, delighted when Sextus announced they would attend The Parilia, the Celebration of the Birth of Rome after which they would return to the house for a private dinner followed by entertainment.

Marcus would have preferred to attend the public open air meal as usual but realized Sextus's dignity as a Senator would preclude his taking part in what could degenerate into a drunken riot.The weather was fine and, for the first time in his life, he could see all the rites of the sacrifice without having to crane his neck.The presence of the VestalVirgins reminded him briefly of his mother but, standing in his new toga with his head respectably covered, he felt every inch the aristocrat confident that nobody would recognize him in his new role of respectable citizen.Then it was back to a dinner of five courses plus several amphorae of excellent wine served in the garden by the light of the traditional bonfires.

During the evening they were entertained by musicians followed by a dancer. In the middle of the dance,Annia, declaring that she was a much better dancer got up, pushed the girl out of the way, and began to dance. Marcus had to admit that she was good.When her dancing became more and more abandoned Sextus got up and went into the house leaving Marcus to enjoy the spectacle.Annia finished her dance with a flourish, declared she was exhausted, and was going to bed. As Marcus sat alone finishing his wine he decided that it had been one of the best Celebrations he could ever remember.

He had hardly recovered when they were off to the grand opening of Pompey's Theatre on the Field of Mars, the first stone Theatre in Rome, as Annia kept telling him, excitedly.

As they made their way to the Theatre by litter Marcus thought of all the times he had been forced out of the way by rich men's litters and how he had cursed them. He had no intention of relinquishing his new-found status if he could help it.

Once seated Marcus enjoyed the luxury of the best seats. Usually he had to put up with a seat so high above the arena that he could hardly see what was going on. The spectacles went on for days and Sextus, as a member of the Senate, had to attend all of them. Marcus enjoyed the plays, Clytemnestra in particular. The sight of 600 mules all in the arena at the same time was an exciting spectacle. He always enjoyed gladiatorial displays and had never had a better view of men being torn to pieces by wild animals. Even so he was shocked by Annia's behaviour. She leapt up and down and got so excited that people were beginning to stare and nudge each other. Sextus became very grim-faced and, when she began to use language which Marcus considered would cause a Centurion to blush, Sextus stood up saying.

"We are going home."

Annia, wild-eyed and dishevelled, began to protest, loudly.

"Take her other arm, Rutilius," Sextus ordered.

Marcus was only too pleased to comply as the last thing he wanted was to draw attention to himself. Eventually between them, they managed to get her safely out of the Theatre.

Once they were inside the house, Sextus retired to his study and Marcus thought it prudent to go to his cubiculum. Keeping out of the way proved to be sensible as, even through the wall, he could hear Annia screaming at the slaves amid the sound of breaking glass.

Marcus was disappointed when Sextus refused to take them to the last day's events when men were to be pitted against elephants, animals Marcus had never seen. He almost went alone but decided there was too much risk of meeting someone he knew as he would have to sit in the less expensive seats. He was even more disappointed when, the next day, he overheard two of the slaves discussing the show. The elephants who, apparently, were huge beasts with two long noses, one at each end, had stampeded and nearly flattened the spectators. He would like to have seen that.

Once the packing for Baeae got under way however, there was no time for entertainment and the house was in chaos. Slaves, chivvied by Lucius, ran in all directions from early morning until well after midnight. Sextus was in the Senate all day and sometimes half the night. Annia kept to her room where she summoned Lucius and countermanded all the orders she had given the day before driving him into a frenzy which he took out on the hapless slaves. Marcus wondered whether they would ever be ready but, eventually, even Annia was satisfied with the preparations.

The night before their departure they dined alone as usual when Sextus startled Marcus by saying

"I have been making enquiries regarding your father and I discover that there are no records of a Tribune called Adituor in the Xth or, indeed, in any other Legion. In fact, there is no record of any Tribune of that name ever having been in the Army."

Sextus looked at Marcus expectantly.

Marcus was flustered. Of course there was no Tribune called Aditour.

"What does it matter, Sextus?" Annia sounded bored. "Anyway his name is not Aditour, it's Rutilius – he told me when he rescued me."

Sextus frowned and looked from Annia to Marcus.

"Is this true?"

Marcus nodded. Sextus asked, pleasantly.

"Tell me, what do you know of Gaius Julius Caesar?"

Marcus was taken aback. Why did Sextus suddenly decide to talk about Caesar? He pulled himself together.

"Only what all Rome knows – he is a great Commander."

He cautiously replied.

"Have you ever met Caesar?"

"No, but I did see him once in the distance." He added, helpfully.

Annia, yawning, began to search in a silver dish for the largest and juiciest grapes.

"I find it strange that you have no male relative. Your mother had a male guardian I presume?"

Panicked at the turn the conversation had taken Marcus replied

"No, Vestal Virgins don't need one."

Annia gasped, a grape halfway to her mouth. In the silence Marcus clearly heard her many bracelets jangle as she dropped the grape back into the dish.

"Your mother was a *Vestal?* Was she buried alive in the Field of Wickness out..."

"Outside the Colline Gate – no, she wasn't. I told you, she died two years ago."

"But that can't be true because if, as you say, your mother was a Vestal she was unchaste and would have to be buried alive, so you could not have been born, so your mother was *not* a Vestal".

And she triumphantly popped a large grape into her mouth.

"But," said Sextus, thoughtfully, "if, on the other hand, she finished her thirty years there was nothing to stop her getting married if she wished."

"She was *not* executed and she *did* complete her thirty years." Marcus insisted. Then added "but she did not get married."

"So you took her name which would give you the name of her family surely?"

"No."

And Marcus told them all that Julia had said on the subject of her family.

"She completely disowned them." Sextus mused, then said, "Where did the name Rutilius come from?"

"Apparently it was the name of a man who was kind to her when she was a child."

"Tell me *exactly* what your mother told you about your father?"

The Senator was watching him keenly. It was evident that, for some reason, his answer was important so he took his time answering.

"One night my mother was leaving the house of the Vestals after visiting the Chief Vestal. This was, of course, after she had left the order."

Sextus nodded but did not speak. He continued to watch Marcus's face as if to read from it whether or not he was telling the truth.

"She told me that, as she was crossing the road on her way home, she stumbled and would have fallen under a horse's hooves had a man not come to her rescue. Then one thing led to another."

"Quite" said Sextus.

Annia, giggling and choking at the same time managed to say.

"How lucky she had left the Vestals or he would have been flogged to death!"

"Yes, very lucky." Sextus agreed. "It could have been somebody she knew perhaps?"

"All I know is that he was a Military Tribune."

"Who does not know he has a son. And your mother did not tell you his full name only that he was called Marcus. Marcus is a pretty common name and could well have been false."

"Yes."

"Did he stay with her for long?"

"I don't think she ever saw him again."

"But she must have tried to find him when she became pregnant?"

"I have no idea, she never discussed it."

Sextus, raising his eyebrows said, "And you say you have no idea who this Tribune was. Perhaps, your mother, like Rhea, was raped by

Mars and instead of producing twins produced you! You don't look like a brother of Romulus and Remus, the founders of Rome, to me!"

Annia, who had been staring at Marcus as if he had suddenly grown two heads, gasped.

"Was she really *raped* by *Mars?"*

"Of course not, Annia," Sextus said, impatiently.

"Then why did you..."

"Be quiet, Annia, I'll explain it to you later."

Annia, looking annoyed, opened her mouth to say something but closed it again as Sextus looked at her in exasperation.

No one spoke for some time then Sextus asked, pleasantly.

"Why did you give us a false name?"

"It must have been the shock of the attack. I lost my memory but its back now."

It sounded thin, even to himself. Surprisingly, Sextus seemed to accept his explanation.

"I see, that would explain it. So your name is Rutilius – but you say your mother changed her name when she left the order, therefore you have no idea what your family name is. As an illegitimate child you are, of course, legally independent and have all the rights of a Roman citizen but, unfortunately, without the help in your career which you would be entitled to expect from your family. A unique position."

He turned to Annia.

"Go to bed, I want to have a word in private with Rutilius."

Reluctantly Annia got up and left the room.

Sextus watched her go then, turning to Marcus, said, "Rutilius, I know we have only just met but you strike me as being reliable and discreet. Am I right?"

Marcus nodded. Yes, he was reliable – at least he felt he *could* be which came to the same thing. As for being discreet, that depended on how much Sextus was prepared to pay.

Sextus continued, "I have been observing you over the past few weeks and have decided to be frank with you. I hope I can rely on your discretion?"

As Marcus nodded he wondered what was coming next.

"I had decided to marry Annia and retire to my villa at Baeae. When I informed my eldest son of this intention he was extremely upset and took it upon himself to investigate Annia's background. He discovered that, originally, she was a slave who was bought by a rich merchant. The old man became besotted with her – she made sure of that I have no doubt. Of course, she would settle for nothing less than marriage and, in order to marry her legally, he had to free her. He quarrelled with his heir, probably over the marriage, and disinherited him in favour of Annia. It was not long before he entered the Underworld and soon after she remarried.

On once more becoming a widow she looked round for another rich victim. If it had not been for the astuteness of my son she would have succeeded. It took him a long time to convince me of the truth as, when I met Annia she was, to all intents and purposes, a respectable widow. She was very cunning and chose as her guardian someone she knew she could rely on not to interfere with her wishes. For a time my son and I were estranged and wanting to prove him wrong I carried out my own investigation only to find that the evidence was irrefutable. Naturally, the marriage will not now take place. That does, however, leave me with a problem. How to get rid of her"

"Can't you tell her what you have discovered and that it is now impossible for you to marry her?"

"That would be the obvious solution. You must understand that I had been in the habit of confiding in my late wife – a model of Roman womanhood who would never have dreamt of discussing my affairs with anyone. Unfortunately, I made the mistake of assuming Annia to be blessed with the same rectitude. The result of this grave error is that she has information which I know she would not hesitate to use against me. She has deliberately cultivated a large circle of female friends, most of whom are wives of influential men and she is astute enough to know that she only has to drop a few timely words into the ear of one of my opponents' wives to discredit me with disastrous consequences.

She is determined to marry me and will stop at nothing, including blackmail, to achieve this aim. So, as you can see, I need to find some way of discarding her. I am almost certain that she is deceiving me and, if I can obtain proof, even immoral Rome will think me justified in casting her off and any rumours she would try to circulate would not be believed. Baeae is far from Rome with just the relaxed atmosphere which would encourage behaviour not tolerated here. I want you to watch her every move. Your arrival at this moment has been so opportune that you must have been sent from the gods! Once I have the proof I need the rest can be accomplished without any fuss and you will not find me ungrateful. If you are successful in this task I may be able to help you in some way when we return."

Marcus understood this to mean that Sextus would become his Patron. A Senator as a Patron – and it had only taken a mugging to bring him to the Senator's attention, he reflected, ruefully.

"But will the man follow her from Rome?"

Marcus asked, doubtfully.

"Oh, I am sure he will."

"You know who it is then?"

"I think so but I don't want to prejudice your investigation."

"I will do all I can to assist you, Senator."

"I am sure you will. Now, take this."

He handed Marcus a money bag saying, "Once your work in Baeae is finished we will talk again. You must have some family, who, I am sure, would be very pleased to acknowledge you. Who knows, you could be a close relation of somebody very influential – then *I* shall be coming to *you* for favours!" he laughed.

"I have often wondered about my father's family. And I must be the grandson of a Senator otherwise my mother could not have become a Vestal. I could be a Severi!" Marcus said, eagerly.

"Or" Sextus interrupted "even a Julian!"

"Caesar's family?" Marcus turned this exciting thought over.

Rising from his couch, Sextus patted Marcus familiarly on the shoulder.

"I expect you want to get some sleep before your journey. I doubt you will get very much before you arrive at Baeae. The roads are not good and the few Inns there are extremely uncomfortable, so I have arranged for you both to be accommodated in private villas along the way. Do not neglect your duty and send me your reports regularly. It is most important that you send them through Lucius and nobody else. Is that clear?"

Marcus nodded.

"And remember this, if you betray my trust you will regret it. Do you understand?"

Once more Marcus nodded. He knew that Sextus meant what he said. He had no intention of jeopardizing what could be a very successful career. "Good. I'll come to Baeae as soon as I can get away from Rome but that may not be for some time."

Once Sextus had gone Marcus decided to take his advice and made his way to his sleeping cubicle.

CHAPTER FOUR

Marcus rose early the next morning eager to leave Rome as soon as possible but, to his annoyance Annia kept him waiting and it was not until late morning that they finally set off, Annia heading the party in a closed litter carried by six slaves and escorted by the four armed ex-gladiators Sextus had insisted on providing to protect them from the highwaymen known to infest the Pontine Marshes. Two luggage wagons completed the party, Marcus following on horseback. Annia insisting on travelling in a closed litter rather than a carriage which he could also share he considered to be pure selfishness as he was an indifferent horseman but, since the only alternative was to ride in one of the wagons with the slaves, he gritted his teeth and mounted the beast. It appeared to be reasonably placid for which he thanked the gods. The crowded streets slowed their progress but eventually they reached the Porta Capena and passing through to the Via Appia were soon out in the country.

Due to their late start they progressed only as far as Aricia where Marcus was relieved to dismount and hand the horse over to a slave with instructions to look after it well. He didn't want anything to happen to it, the thought of having to ride a livelier animal filled him with horror.

Annia was not pleased to be informed by Lucius, who had gone on ahead to warn the villa of their arrival, that only the house slaves were in occupation. Marcus, on the other hand, was not at all sorry. He did not want to exert himself being pleasant to people, all he wanted was a visit to the bath suite followed by a massage to ease away his stiffness.

After a very relaxing bath and a change of tunic he joined Annia for an indifferent dinner which was accompanied by a wine his newly educated taste buds told him was definitely not a Falernian. He found it difficult to enjoy his food as Annia kept up a running commentary on the villa's decor, furniture, food and the discipline of the slaves all of which she found wanting. Eventually, having exhausted things to complain about, she turned her attention to Marcus and made it clear she would not object to his providing her with some diversion.

Self-preservation always being Marcus's first priority, he did not respond. He wasn't going to run the risk of Lucius, who seemed to be keeping a very close eye on them both, informing Sextus. Sulking, she went alone to her bed leaving Marcus to finish his wine and reflect on the day.

This set the pattern for the journey, a long hot day through marshes and narrow mountain passes. Once the road ran along a viaduct above a precipice. Marcus looked down, gulped, shut his eyes and let the horse do the rest. After the novelty of being out of the City wore off it all became a blur, one forest, marsh, vineyard or mountain looking very much like another. The only respite was when they stopped for the night. Marcus thanked the gods that as most of the villas' owners were Roman officials of one kind or another they were away in Rome leaving only a few slaves in residence.

Annia only came to life at dinner especially when they had a hostess whom she could regale with her opinions of the latest fashions in Rome, at the same time managing to convey the lack of sophistication found outside that city. Finding the conversation boring, Marcus invariably excused himself and retired to his sleeping cubicle.

The further they got from Rome the more Annia's temper deteriorated which she took out on her personal slave. Several times he found the girl sobbing in a corner and once, as she was climbing into one of the luggage wagons, he saw a livid handprint on her face.

He soon became bored with the journey but found some diversion in watching their burly escort who kept up a steady pace all day long never appearing tired. At the end of the day they would exercise in the villa courtyard before disappearing into the slave quarters. They kept themselves to themselves and rarely spoke to anyone other than each other.

Marcus was annoyed when he discovered that Lucius had been put in charge of the travel arrangements rather than himself. Annia, however, seemed quite happy with the situation. Marcus was surprised at the amount of freedom she allowed the slave but concluded that she was lazy and Lucius was Sextus's slave after all. He had to admit that Lucius was extremely efficient, easily dealing with such problems as the horde of watermen at Forum of Appius who were very insistent that they took the canal through the Pontine Marshes to avoid the highwaymen. When Marcus questioned his decision, Lucius told him.

"My Master gave me specific instructions. Besides, the watermen are even bigger rogues than the highwaymen. The gladiators can deal with any trouble on dry land but it would not be so easy on water."

When they finally ventured into the marshes there were no highwaymen in evidence only plenty of mosquitoes. Annia, being in a closed litter, was not too badly bitten although she complained loudly but Marcus, in spite of wearing a light cloak with a cloth round his head and face, was bitten very severely round his eyes which of necessity he had to keep uncovered. His eyelids were so badly swollen that Lucius took pity on him and, when they stopped that evening, sent a slave to his room with a salve which soothed his eyelids enough to enable him to get some sleep.

On reaching Cumae they found the villa full of visitors.

Their host, Lucius Annius Fabianus, seemed a pleasant enough fellow.

"The Senator and I are old friends. I welcome you to my villa. Please treat it as your own." He told them.

The slave who showed Marcus to his cubiculum informed him that he would come and conduct him to the bath suite before dinner.

Later, when he entered the triclinium, he found the other guests already assembled and as he took the only vacant place Fabianus interrupted his conversation to say.

"There you are, Rutilius."

The man on the couch opposite Marcus watched him as he settled himself then asked

"Your name is?"

"Marcus Rutilius."

"From Rome." Fabianus added.

The man nodded in acknowledgement and resumed his conversation with the man next to him.

The meal was excellent consisting of several meat dishes, fish, poultry, some vegetables which he had never seen before, and fruit. The wine was not first class but Marcus decided it was drinkable.

Annia was in her element during dinner as the women were eager to hear about the latest fashions and the gossip from Rome. The men discussed the latest move by the Senate to deprive Caesar of his Command of the Legions and wondered what he would do. The man on the couch opposite Marcus said something to his companion who shook his head and laid a hand on his arm. The man, who was clearly in the first stages of intoxication, shook the hand off with a bad-tempered gesture and loudly asked.

"Rutilius, where do you stand on this Caesar/Pompey question?"

He could feel a sudden tension as the other men stopped talking and listened attentively. For some reason they were eager to hear what he had to say. Only the chatter of the women broke the silence. "Neither – I have no interest in politics."

"But you must have," the man persisted. "You are for Caesar, you *must* be – admit it!"

"Leave it, Titus. Be prudent for once." Their host intervened.

Subsiding, muttering, the man held out his goblet for a slave to fill.

Feeling that he had missed something important but not sure what, Marcus gave up trying to work it out and listened instead to a stout matron informing Annia of the merits of Cumae to the detriment of Rome.

"Of course we have the famous Sibyl. You must have heard of her – even in Rome." Annia sniffed. "She is the only Sibyl to live in a cave you know and her predictions are *never* wrong. You must visit her!"

"I think I would rather not," Annia replied. "In any case we are moving on tomorrow."

"But, my dear, you can't come all this way and not look round Cumae at least. We have some excellent shops. Our jewellery is famous. Then, if you don't want to visit the cave, there is the lake and the …"

Annia showed more interest once shops were mentioned.

"Well perhaps we could spend another day and I could visit the shops. What do you think, Marcus?"

Marcus felt a flutter of excitement. A Sibyl – predictions! A prediction from the Sibyl would confirm what he had always suspected – that he *was* destined for great things!

"I would like to consult the Sibyl."

"Excellent idea and while you are with the Sibyl I will show Annia the sights of Cumae. Better than anything in Rome I can assure you!"

The stout matron gushed.

Upon consulting Fabianus Marcus discovered that, although not far from the Villa, the cave could only be reached through dense woods followed by a steep climb up a hill.

"What rites should I perform and what about a sacrifice?" Marcus asked.

"The Sibyl has been silent for some time I am afraid."

Fabianus informed him.

"But I must consult the Sibyl – she is the only one who can tell me how to attain my true destiny. Jupiter Optimus Maximus himself told me to consult her."

Well, he was sure Jupiter had meant to, he just hadn't got round to it.

"Did he! Jupiter eh! Well we must not go against *him!* Let me consult my Chief Household Slave."

Marcus watched as Fabianus took the slave aside and seemed to be giving him detailed instructions. Although he could not hear what was being said, Fabianus must have referred to himself as, at one point, the slave turned, looked at him and smiled. Marcus smiled back – the man had probably never seen anyone who was in contact with Jupiter before. Once the slave had left Fabianus rejoined Marcus.

"Everything has been arranged. You will be taken to the cave so that you can consult the Sibyl. I am sure that she will speak to you as you have the ear of Jupiter Optimus Maximus himself. My Chief Household Slave will go with you and one of the other slaves will take some strips of cloth to wind round your legs before you enter the woods otherwise they will be torn to shreds. I should wear a tunic, not a toga, togas are not worn in the country except on very formal occasions. Not very practical."

Accordingly, the next day, in great excitement, Marcus, accompanied by the two centurions for protection, the Chief Household Slave as guide and a slave carrying torches to light the cave, strips of cloth for their legs and some food set off through the woods, along a gulley and up a steep and difficult path to the wedge-shaped cave entrance where the Chief Household slave lit and handed him a torch, indicating that he was to go in alone.

He entered a narrow tunnel, the roof high above his head, on his left a rock face on which the light of the torch cast gigantic shadows, on his right apertures at intervals along the side of the tunnel giving a patchy light. It felt cold and dank and he shivered partly in fear and partly with excitement. The tunnel seemed to go on for ever then it sloped downwards and he came to a large dark chamber. He could go no further. All was silent. There was no sign of the Sibyl. As he stood, feeling more and more uneasy, he thought he heard a voice coming from somewhere above him.

"Yes?"

He asked, tentatively taking a few steps forward.

"Who comes?"

The voice sounded gravelly – almost masculine which puzzled him – the Sibyl was a woman but then he remembered that she was old – some said as much as 400 years.

Holding the torch high Marcus peered into the gloom but could see nothing.

"Marcus Rutilius." His voice sounded too loud.

"Why do you consult the Sibyl, Marcus Rutilius?"

"I wish to know my destiny," he whispered.

"Your destiny is one day to become a great man of Rome!" came the reply.

Marcus could hardly speak for excitement. So he was destined for great things! He had to know more.

"When will this day come?"

The voice of the Sibyl seemed to be fading away and Marcus had to stretch his ears to catch the words.

"The oracle has spoken. If the words of the oracle are divulged to any other living person misfortune will follow."

Then silence.

He waited but, to his disappointment, there were no more revelations and the torch being on the point of going out leaving him in darkness, he made his way out of the cave and stood in the entrance, blinking in the bright sunlight.

The Chief Household slave joined him.

"Did the Sibyl speak to you, Master?" he enquired.

"Yes, she did."

The slave assumed an expression of awe.

"She has not spoken in many years. My Master was right – you *are* special!"

Marcus drew himself up.

"I must return to the villa and think over what the Sibyl has divulged." He stated, importantly.

On the way back to the villa Marcus kept his distance from the slaves. He could hear them whispering together behind him. One of the gladiators laughed and turning, Marcus frowned at him. The man was swift to apologize.

"Sorry, Master – I did not mean to interrupt your Honour's thoughts."

Nodding in acknowledgement, Marcus continued his stately walk.

As soon as they arrived at the villa the gladiators disappeared into the slave quarters.

Marcus, accompanied by the Chief Household Slave, entered the Atrium where Fabianus greeted him with the words.

"Did the Sibyl speak to you, Rutilius?"

"Yes, but I have been warned not to repeat what she said."

"Then of course you must not. Excuse me I must give my Chief Household slave some instructions."

Marcus watched Fabianus and the slave walk away. Fabianus appeared to ask the slave a question. The reply seemed to amuse him. These urban Romans had no sense of dignity, Marcus decided and went through the atrium and into the main reception room where he found Annia.

"There you are," She said, crossly.

"I hope you have had a better day than I have. That wretched woman dragged me all round Cumae. Now my feet hurt and my head aches. Well, what did the Sibyl say?"

"I have been told not to say," Marcus rather pompously replied.

Annia tried sulks, cajolings and tantrums but he remained resolute. He was not going to risk such a brilliant destiny for the sake of a woman's curiosity! Eventually Annia flounced out of the room saying she did not believe that the Sibyl had said anything to him at all.

Marcus breathed a sigh of relief when she had gone, he was very glad that the following day would see them at Baeae, the journey over and, thank Hercules, he could finally bid farewell to his horse.

They arrived at the villa just before dark. It was of modest size although larger than the house in Rome. His sleeping cubicle, however, was very nicely decorated; the walls painted with garden scenes, the floor covered with a bright mosaic and the bed looked comfortable. He was going to enjoy his stay here. As it would not last for ever he was determined to make the most of it.

Exhausted after the long journey, he retired immediately after dinner. He woke early the next morning feeling much better and eager to explore. Upon enquiry, Lucius informed him that "The Mistress is still resting."

Going out onto the terrace which ran the whole width of the villa he enjoyed the view of the sea which was just visible over the top of the high wall surrounding the property and thought over the Sibyl's words. What did she mean by "one day?" How soon would it be? How would it happen? He could think of no possible answers so he went down into the garden where several slaves were working.

Approaching a slave tending one of the rectangular flower beds he asked, "Who is the Subvillicus?"

"Our Supervisor is Stronnius. He's over there".

The slave waved his hoe in the direction of a man watching two slaves putting small statues of various animals, gods and goddesses on plinths placed in front of each of the large trees which ran down both sides of the garden.

"Stronnius?"

Stronnius checked that a statue of Hercules was exactly where he wanted it before turning.

"I am Stronnius."

Marcus spent some time talking to the overseer. He could be useful. How, he was not sure at the moment. Marcus always liked to know who he could use if the occasion arose and garden slaves usually knew most of the household's movements. He discovered that Sextus was more interested in the gardens than the villa and that one day he intended retiring to the villa in order to cultivate his garden.

Marcus asked, "Bit of a nuisance is he? Stands in the garden giving orders?"

"No, he is a very good Master. He loves his garden. Puts on an old tunic and works with the rest of us. Makes sure we have everything necessary to do the work. Come and see this."

He led the way to a wooden door set into the terrace wall. Reaching inside his tunic he produced a key attached to a leather thong round his neck. Unlocking the door he stepped aside so that Marcus could enter.

"The Master had the cryptoporticus enlarged into a workroom for us. As you can see, it has been fully stocked with tools." Stronnius said, proudly.

Marcus looked round with interest. This could be a very good place to conceal himself if necessary. The interior was illuminated by grilled apertures set high up in the wall enabling him to see that the whole length of the narrow space under the terrace had been turned into a working area. Down one wall were hooks on which gleaming forks, spades, hoes, pruning hooks, shears, and every tool likely to be required for the cultivation of a garden hung. Along the other side of the storage space were stacked flower pots, empty wooden trays, and clean sacks.

"This is very impressive, Stronnius. These tools look expensive. I hope you have good security?"

"Oh yes, the Master is strict about that. He is a very private man. You will notice the shards on the top of the wall? We even had to import mature trees to put round the garden although the wall is so high."

"If you don't want anyone poking round this nice storage space and deciding it would be a useful place in which to keep food cool I suggest you keep the key somewhere safe."

"Oh, the key is quite safe, Master. It never leaves me."

Once outside Marcus strolled round looking at the flowers while Stronnius went back to supervising the sweating slaves. Marcus watched them for a while then, when he was sure he was not observed, tried the door in the garden wall. It was locked. He was not dismayed. He had come across locked garden doors before. The key was always "hidden" close by. No one wants to go round looking for a garden door key when they fancy a short stroll. Noticing a small, empty, niche, probably intended for a statue, he ran his hand round the inside but it was empty. Running his hand along the wall on the other side of the door he immediately found a large key suspended on a nail. Feeling that he had made enough progress for one morning he made his way back on to the terrace where he found Lucius in the summer dining room supervising the setting out of a light meal.

Annia appeared soon afterwards only to disappear to her room immediately after she had eaten saying the heat exhausted her. It *was* hot and Marcus felt sleepy so he retired to his room where he lay on his bed trying to work out his next move. By the time he fell asleep the only thing he was sure of was that he didn't have a next move.

He woke in time to visit the villa's bath suite before dinner. Although small in scale everything available in the public baths in Rome was here – the changing room, the hot bath, the cold plunge – and he had it all to himself! Best of all were the well-trained slaves who scraped the dirt off him with strigils and massaged him with oils. Then, feeling every inch a "great man", he enjoyed an excellent dinner which included oysters fresh from Lake Lucinus and Sextus's favourite Falernian, of which, by the way Lucius kept filling his goblet, Sextus had a large stock.

Unusually, Marcus woke late the next morning and when he reached the terrace he found Annia already there with Lucius hovering nearby as usual.

"You slept well, Marcus?" Annia asked.

"Very well and I still feel tired. It must have been the wine at dinner."

"It is more likely to be the sea air. It has that effect if you are not used to it. Don't you agree, Lucius?"

"Yes, Mistress." Annia rose.

"I intend to inspect the villa this morning, Marcus, and I should like you to come with me."

She handed Lucius a writing tablet and stylus

"Take notes, there will probably be some alterations."

"Shouldn't you wait until Sextus arrives?" Marcus asked.

"His ideas are so old-fashioned and he has no idea how a modern villa should be decorated. Anyway I am sure he will approve of any improvements I decide to make." Annia replied, dimissively.

Marcus was not so sure about that but decided it would do no harm to humour her – at least he would know where she was.

They made their way to the atrium where Annia gazed round the walls in dismay.

"This is dreadful. There are too many garden scenes. I like mythological scenes, it will have to be repainted. It is the central hall after all."

"It would be very expensive to repaint," Marcus pointed out.

"Sextus can afford it and it is what I want. Stop being so grumpy, Marcus."

She gazed up at the opening in the roof with its animal shaped waterspouts then at the wide, shallow white marble basin below empty of water and filled with rubbish.

"Lucius, the impluvium must be cleaned out immediately or the rainwater will go to waste, make a note."

"Yes, Mistress."

They continued their slow progress through all the rooms, Annia deciding on sweeping changes in each one. She disliked the dining room decoration and decreed the red paint with black panels had to go to be replaced by white paint. And so it was through the rest of the villa.

When they had thoroughly inspected the private rooms Marcus asked, innocently.

"Will you be inspecting the slave quarters?"

"Certainly not! Whatever gave you the idea that I know of slave quarters?"

Marcus smiled at her.

"Nothing, I'm sure."

Annia gave him a sharp look which he returned with a steady gaze.

"I think I will take an inventory of the furniture. Come, Lucius."

Sensing that he had been dismissed, Marcus escaped to the garden where he found Stronnius inspecting the fishpond fountain.

"I think the Mistress intends to inspect the gardens next, Stronnius, so perhaps you had better get the fountain working."

"The Master has given full instructions about the gardens and they did *not* include anyone other than himself interfering as I told Lucius this morning."

"You and Lucius don't get on then?"

Yanking up a piece of weed with unnecessary force Stronnius replied

"Can't say that we do. As I told him this morning he can do what he likes in the house. The gardens are *my* responsibility. Coming here from Rome, acting as if he is the Master…"

Leaving him muttering to himself as he massacred yet more weed, Marcus went back into the house to find that Annia had taken to her bed, exhausted.

CHAPTER FIVE

For several days Annia had been lamenting the lack of anyone interesting in Baeae declaring that the place was dead and she was bored. Then, suddenly, people began to arrive like swallows in summer and she forgot about inspecting the gardens. When Marcus reminded her she snapped

"The gardens can wait. I'm sure whats-his-name the Supervisor has everything under control. I want to enjoy myself, besides, I must go into Puteoli and buy some decent clothes. I have nothing to wear. Although what I shall find I don't know, this is not Rome after all."

"As this is not Rome does it matter what you wear?" Marcus asked.

"Of course it matters! You never know who you will meet here!"

Marcus yawned – as usual he found all this talk of female clothing extremely boring and as soon as he was able he escaped to the garden to talk to Stronnius. One of the garden slaves pointed to the cryptoporticus but when he went in he looked in vain for the Supervisor. He was just about to leave when he saw him sitting hunched in a corner, his knees drawn up and his head down on his folded arms. He did not move until Marcus touched him.

"Stronnius? Are you ill?"

Marcus was concerned. If Stronnius was really ill he would not be much help to him.

Stronnius wearily raised his head.

"No, I'm not ill."

"Then what's the matter with you?" Marcus asked, impatiently. He was surprised at Stronnius's sudden descent into depression. He could not see what he had to be depressed about.

Stronnius looked at Marcus as though wondering whether or not to trust him, then said, "The Master has never had guests before, he likes his solitude. He once told me that he did not want his villa tainted with the stink of Rome. He refuses to see any clients even when they travel from Rome so I don't understand why he has allowed anyone to come here especially in his absence."

Thinking it best to change the subject Marcus asked, "How did you end up here?"

"The Master was on an inspection tour for the Senate and came to the mine where I worked. For some reason he decided to buy me. I know that I'm very lucky, he is a good Master and has promised to free me when the gardens are finished."

"Where were you captured?"

"In Gaul, ten years ago."

"Did you have a family?"

"Yes, a wife and four children. I don't know what happened to them. They could be dead for all I know. All I have thought about for the last ten years is how to get back to Gaul and look for them. I'm tired of waiting. I've been a slave long enough. I want to be a free man again. That's why I'm so worried that the Master will change his mind about freeing me."

"And he has promised to free you once the gardens are finished?"

"Yes."

"How long will that take?"

"We've only just begun. Besides, the Master may decide he doesn't like the effect after all and begin all over again. Also – "

"Yes?"

"Also if he marries his wife is bound to make changes and he must be thinking of marrying again otherwise why has a woman come?" Stronnius said, in a rush.

Marcus was tempted to assure Stronnius that Sextus had no intention of getting married but did not know if he could trust the slave so decided against it. Instead he said, "Try not to worry."

Shaking his head, Stronnius made no answer and put his head down on his arms once more. Marcus could think of nothing to say so he left the workroom pulling the door shut behind him.

"Stronnius is busy and does not wish to be disturbed," he told the slave who had directed him.

"I understand, Master. I'll look after him."

As he walked away, Marcus was turning over what Stronnius had told him. He had never thought about it before but now realized that he had always taken it for granted that the Roman way of life was the most civilized and the conquered peoples grateful to be made part of it. He had never had any reason to question this until now. How would *he* react to being treated as a slave? Why worry about it he told himself and went in to dinner thanking Jupiter Optimus Maximus that, with his gift for survival, the chances of his becoming a slave were nil.

The fine weather broke that night in a spectacular thunderstorm. The rain, cascading from the compluvium waterspouts into the newly cleaned impluvium below made a noise like a waterfall which, together with the crack of the thunder, kept Marcus awake half the night and he felt very tired the next morning.

The rain prevented Annia from going to Puteoli to raid the dress shops as she had intended which made her extremely bad-tempered. She shouted at the slaves just for being in the room. As the rain had shown no sign of easing by mid-afternoon, Marcus decided to go to the bath suite and luxuriate for an hour or two before dinner. As he made his way through the Atrium he saw that the rain had eased at last which enabled him to hear the murmur of voices coming from behind a wooden screen drawn across the entrance to the triclinium. Curious why anyone should be in the dining hall at that time of day he went closer and put his ear to a crack in one of the panels.

"Have you done as I told you?" Annia's voice.

Marcus could faintly hear a man's voice as if he were keeping his voice low. Annia's, on the other hand, was at normal pitch.

"I'll come to you later, never fear."

She sounded conciliatory.

A low murmur in reply.

"We must not be impatient otherwise all our plans will be ruined. I'll tell you when it is safe to act," she replied, crisply.

Marcus pressed his ear even closer to the panel, he wanted to hear what the man was saying. Could this be the man from Rome?

"Master?"

Marcus jumped – he had been so intent on listening that he had not been aware that a slave had come through the Atrium. Mentally consigning the woman to the netherworld, Marcus, acting as if he was about to enter the room slid open the wooden doors and entered the room where he found Annia lying on a dining couch eating fruit from a silver dish and Lucius in the act of handing her a goblet of wine.

"Is that all, Mistress?"

"Yes, Lucius. What do you want, Marcus?"

"I came to tell you that I think the rain has eased."

"Well, it's too late to go out now, isn't it?" Annia replied, crossly.

"I thought I heard voices. Have you had a visitor?" Marcus casually enquired.

"Visitor? Oh, you mean the wall-painter. I was arranging an appointment to go and see some of his work."

Marcus looked round the room.

"I don't see him?"

"Of course you don't. He left before you came in. Why are you so interested in a wall-painter?" she asked, suspiciously.

"Oh, no reason. I think I'll visit the bath suite," Marcus hastily replied and backed towards the door.

Annia not bothering to reply, he made his escape. While the bath slaves removed his dirt and massaged him he pondered on what he had heard. He *had* heard a man's voice. How could the man have left without him seeing him? A bizarre thought struck him – perhaps Annia and Lucius – no, impossible, even Annia would not be so stupid as to stoop to a slave right under Sextus's roof especially if she planned marriage. Besides, slaves talked. No, there was no way they could keep it secret. He dismissed the thought. If only that stupid slave had not come along at that moment he might have been able to hear what the man was saying.

That evening at dinner Annia, declaring that the food was inedible and probably poisoned, snatched the tray out of the serving slave's hands and threw it across the room, hitting another slave, missing Lucius by inches and splattering the wall with fish sauce. Having screamed that she would make sure they were all sold, she stormed out of the triclinium.

Marcus ordered the slaves to clear up the mess and prepare him fresh food. Whilst he waited for it to appear he motioned to a slave to pour him some wine. Lucius, who was in attendance as usual, waved the slave aside and brought the wine himself. Marcus moodily held out his goblet to be filled. As he drank he reflected that he would be doing not only Sextus but the slaves a favour if he could find some evidence that would enable Sextus to rid himself of Annia and her tantrums.

The rain began again early the next day. Annia and Marcus were barely speaking. He was feeling bored with nobody to talk to and had intended going to see how Stronnius was but, the idea of getting wet not appealing to him, he did not bother. Instead he wandered through the villa until he found Sextus's excellent library, the rectangular niches of which contained wooden chests full of scrolls. Lying on the reading couch, he alternately read and went over the information he had gathered so far – which, if he was honest, was non-existent. He had to come up with something, his future could depend on it. If only that thrice-cursed slave had not appeared!

The next afternoon Marcus was on his way to Sextus's library, intending to finish reading Cato's History, when he was accosted by the garden slave who seemed to be Stronnius's friend.

"Master!" the slave hissed.

"What are you doing here? Garden slaves are not allowed in the house – you know that. You had better go, the Mistress is in a very bad mood and will probably have you whipped. Tell Stronnius I'll come and see him presently."

"Master, you don't understand."

The slave stood, wringing his hands, and to his surprise, Marcus thought he saw tears in his eyes.

Greatly intrigued, Marcus bundled him into the library.

The slave stood awkwardly, first on one foot then the other as if afraid that, by standing on both feet he would damage the magnificent floor mosaic. Probably never been inside the house before, Marcus decided. Something very serious must have happened. If he could only calm the man down he might learn what the trouble was. Briskly he asked

"What is so serious that you risk a whipping?"

"Its Stronnius, Master, he's run away and I don't know what to do. You have been so kind to him and I couldn't think of anyone else to ask for help."

The slave looked at him expectantly. Marcus had no idea what to do. He thought for a moment and then asked

"Where do *you* think he has gone?"

"I am sure that he is making his way to Puteoli to find a ship to take him back to Gaul."

Marcus pondered, then said, "I notice that none of you wear slave collars. Are any of you branded?"

"No, the Master said he did not need to as he trusted us not to run away."

"So, if Stronnius does manage to get to Puteoli he will be able to get a ship without anyone knowing he is a runaway slave. How long has he been gone?"

"Only a few hours. He stayed in the workroom for a long time. He has been like this before so I thought he would come to himself but when one of the other slaves said he had seen him by the gate in the wall I went to look in the workroom but he wasn't there or anywhere in the garden. This is the first time he has run away. I didn't know what to do Master, so I came to you."

"Will this other slave tell anyone?"

"No, Master, none of the garden slaves will betray him, we all stick together."

"How long do you think it will be before he is missed?"

The slave considered.

"If one of the kitchen slaves needs to see him about some garden produce and he is missing they might tell Lucius."

Marcus made up his mind. These garden slaves could be useful allies. Stronnius had access to the cryptoporticus room and might be persuaded to turn a blind eye to someone coming and going by the garden door especially at night so he needed to get him back.

"Meet me by the garden door. I won't be long."

Opening the door he checked the corridor. Finding it empty, he beckoned to the slave who scuttled off.

As he took his weatherproof cape from the wooden cupboard in his sleeping cubicle Marcus wondered what he was getting himself into.

It had stopped raining but the cloud was very heavy which worked to their advantage. Only slaves would be out on a day like this.

Marcus and the slave whose name, he discovered, was Aulus, walked along peering everywhere for signs of Stronnius. Marcus asked Aulus questions which he answered reluctantly at first but, with Marcus's encouragement, he told him his story. He had been born into slavery and knew no other life. He had no ambition to be free, he had food every day, a slave girl whenever he wanted one and a roof over his head. He could, however, understand how Stronnius felt.

"If I was captured and taken away from my home here I would want to get away." He told Marcus.

"You regard this as your home?"

"Oh yes, it is a good life. If only Lucius was not the Chief Household slave I would be happy."

He stopped and put a hand to his mouth in horror.

"You won't report me to Lucius will you, Master?" He pleaded.

"No. Is there no way to get rid of him? Surely you slaves know all the secrets of the household? There must be *something* Lucius does not want discovered? An arrangement with suppliers. A few denarii on the bill, or a fee for using certain merchants, something like that. It's not unusual for a slave to steal from his master in order to get enough money together to buy his freedom."

"I think there is something that the household slaves know about but they don't talk about it, they're all too frightened."

"How long has your Master owned Lucius?"

"Since Lucius was a child. Lucius is like me, he was born into slavery. He always talks to us about the Master as if he is totally in his confidence. Master, look!"

Marcus looked to where Aulus pointed and saw a familiar figure coming towards them. Stronnius saw them at the same time and, even before he was up to them, called

"I've been very stupid, Master. Please help me to get back before I'm missed, don't tell my Master."

The slave's usual confident manner had completely deserted him, and he was shaking.

"I will help you but we must get back as quickly as we can. Walk behind me the pair of you then, if we meet anyone, it will look as if I am out for a walk with a pair of slaves to protect me."

As they retraced their steps, the rain recommenced. Marcus pulled his hood further over his head and hoped all this was going to be worth his while.

As they walked, Stronnius told them how he had suddenly found life intolerable and, almost before he knew what he was doing, he was on the road to Puteoli to find a ship but he had not gone more than four or five miles before he realized how foolish it would be to throw away the chance of being made free in a few years time. The alternative was to spend the rest of his life dodging slave-hunters and, if caught, probably crucified. Even Sextus would not be able to save him. As a member of the Senate, Sextus would have to uphold the law and one of Sextus's slaves running away would be all the other slave-owners needed to persecute their slaves even more severely. He could not be responsible for doing that. Besides, Sextus had been very good to him, he could not let him down. He knew the Senator to be an honourable man who would stick to his word to free him, all he had to do was wait.

As they came within sight of the Villa, Stronnius said, "Thank you, Master, for coming after me. Anything I can do for you just ask, anything at all."

This was what Marcus had been hoping for. He did not go running after slaves in the rain without expecting something in return.

"I will certainly let you know when there is anything you can do. Now you had better go on ahead and I will come after you as if I have been for a walk on my own."

That way if they were seen he could not be implicated.

As it was growing dark it was easy for the slaves to slip in by the garden door and through to the slave quarters at the back of the Villa. Waiting until he was sure they were well inside Marcus walked into the house where he found Annia in the triclinium. Not bothering to look up from the wild fowl she was dismembering she snapped

"Where have you been? I don't keep slaves to cook dinner for people who are late."

"I went for a walk, got lost, and then it rained. I'll change and join you." He said, pleasantly.

Annia did not bother to reply.

He was distracted all evening trying to work out how he could use the slave's gratitude to his advantage. Upon Annia becoming annoyed by his inattention he said his long walk had exhausted him and that he would go to bed. As he began to leave the room she called him back.

"By the way, I'll be going into Puteoli tomorrow whether it rains or not."

"Of course, you have to see the wall-painter."

"Wall-painter? Oh, yes, of course, the wall-painter. I've decided to take your advice and wait until Sextus arrives and discuss it with him before I see the wall-painter."

"In that case I'll come with you."

"No, you'll only be bored. I'm going to dress shops and probably the jewellers – unless, of course, you would like to buy me something?"

Marcus shook his head.

"No, I thought not."

Somehow he must follow her. Perhaps Stronnius would have access to a wagon or at least know how he could procure one.

The next morning was fine and for once he was not feeling heavy-headed so was up early to put his problem to Stronnius. During the night Marcus had thought carefully about taking Stronnius fully into his confidence and, in the end, decided to risk it and found the Supervisor only too eager to do anything short of murder that would prevent Sextus from getting married.

"We usually take the oxcart in to town tomorrow but nobody will question it if we go today. It would be better if Aulus picks you up on the road in case anyone is watching. I will tell him everything."

"I don't know about that. The fewer people who know about this the better. I'm sure your Master would not want his business discussed by his slaves!"

"If I tell Aulus not to tell anyone about it he won't. I trust him completely, Master. When I was brought here I was very ill. Work in a mine with very little food had nearly killed me and the master told Aulus to look after me. If it had not been for Aulus I would probably be dead."

Marcus reluctantly agreed but, as a precaution, ordered Stronnius to only tell the slave what it was necessary for him to know.

Just as Marcus finished making his arrangements he looked round to find Annia had come into the garden. He was afraid she had overheard their conversation but she appeared to be inspecting the fish pond. She beckoned Stronnius over to her.

"Why are there no fish in this pond?" she demanded.

"The Master has not yet given me any orders regarding the stocking of the pond."

Stronnius informed her, politely.

"Mistress, you address me as *Mistress* in future or I will have you flogged!"

Stronnius drew himself up. Marcus suddenly realised how large he was. He hoped he was not going to do anything rash, but he only said, "Yes, Mistress."

"Well, don't forget. Go about your business."

"Yes, Mistress."

Annia watched him go.

"That slave is insolent. After Sextus and I are married I shall get rid of him. Now, Marcus, what will you do while I'm gone?"

"I shall spend the day in the library."

As soon as Annia had departed in her litter Marcus, after giving orders that he was not to be disturbed, made sure he was seen making his way to the library where he waited just inside the door until he was sure no slaves were in evidence then made his way down the corridor and through the Atrium to the garden considering himself very fortunate in not encountering any slaves.

Once outside the Villa he walked briskly up the road until Aulus and the cart caught up with him.

"I saw the Mistress's litter leave, we are not far behind. I can help you, Master, the Mistress does not know me. She has never even spoken to me. I could report back to you."

Marcus turned the suggestion over. Aulus certainly had a point but was he trustworthy? He only had Stronnius's word for it which was undoubtedly coloured by the fact that Aulus had nursed him back to health. He might just spend the time in a tavern and give Marcus a false report. Besides he would probably expect to be paid.

"Thank you all the same, Aulus but it is *my* job, and I know what I'm doing."

Aulus looked disappointed but did not argue.

When they reached Puteoli the traffic was so heavy that they nearly lost the litter in the press. Fortunately, it had to stop when Annia thrust her head through the curtains and screamed at the slaves to be more careful.

After instructing Aulus to keep him in sight he climbed down from the cart and followed her on foot. Annia entered a dress shop and he picked up a glass vase from a nearby stall pretending to study it closely. The stallholder, becoming suspicious when some considerable time had elapsed without any sign of Marcus purchasing the item, told him to "Either buy the goods or leave them alone."

"I don't want your Egyptian rubbish – here, catch!"

Marcus threw the vase at the man and walked away nearly colliding with Annia coming out of the shop followed by a slave carrying parcels. For a moment he thought she had seen him but she turned to instruct the slave to "Be careful with those parcels. If you drop one I will have you whipped!"

Marcus followed Annia from shop to shop. So far she had done nothing to arouse suspicion. Once she seemed to look straight at him where he was standing on the other side of the road and he was relieved when she gave no sign that she had seen him through the crowd. By midday he was hot and tired. Finally, when he was sure she had been to every shop in Puteoli, she called for her litter slaves to take her back to Baeae.

Beckoning Aulus, he climbed into the cart. Although Aulus pressed him to tell him what he had discovered Marcus only answered the slave's questions in monosyllables and they followed her back to the Villa in silence where Marcus thanked Aulus, descended from the cart and made his way to the bath suite.

After dinner that evening he went to the library, found writing tablet and stylus and wrote his first report to Sextus telling him that, so far, Annia had shown no signs of any impropriety. For some time he debated whether or not to mention the half conversation he had overheard but decided there was not sufficient evidence to make it worthwhile. As he was finishing Lucius appeared, as if by magic, at his elbow.

"This is an urgent letter for Sextus Caius Quintilius, make sure it is sent to Rome immediately."

"Yes, Master. Shall I seal it for you?"

"No, I'll do that."

After sealing the letter Marcus gave it to the slave repeating that it was extremely urgent.

"Yes, Master. The Master's private courier will take it to Rome immediately."

Feeling that he had made a good start Marcus went to bed, satisfied that, although Annia had not betrayed herself so far, it was only a matter of time and patience.

Having bought her clothes Annia decided to have a good time. She went for boat trips, to concerts, and visited temples always insisting that Marcus go with her. She never gave the slightest hint that she would rather go alone. On one occasion when Marcus, deciding that she was never going to do anything worth reporting, said he would rather stay at home, she pointed out that, as he had agreed to act as her protector, he had no choice.

He always watched her very closely ready to note the slightest sign of her favouring any man above another or spending time alone with anyone but the only man she spent time with was himself and he was aware that gossip was circulating round Baeae regarding their relationship.

Stronnius was also working on his behalf. He met Marcus late each night in the cryptoporticus to report on his progress. Marcus was dismayed that, although Stronnius had talked to as many slaves from the other villas as he could he had discovered nothing, the only thing he could say with any certainty was that there was something going on that the house slaves knew about but not one of them would tell him what it was. Marcus told him to try harder, he had to have something to report to Sextus soon or he could forget any patronage from Sextus or anyone else.

Then, at dinner one evening, Annia announced that she had been invited to visit some ladies in the neighbourhood whom she had met in one of the Puteoli dress shops.

"You don't need to come, Marcus, as this is a strictly female affair – we want to talk of the Bona Dea who, as you must know, is sacred only to women so, of course, you are not welcome. Lucius will come with me for protection and wait outside with the litter slaves – unless, of course, you are prepared to do the same?"

"Of course not – *I* am not a slave!"

Was this the breakthrough he had been waiting for? Not entirely believing the Bona Dea story Marcus decided to follow, see which house she visited then get Stronnius to find out from their garden slaves who lived there. It should be easy enough, all slaves gossiped about their Masters at every opportunity. He would have liked Stronnius's help but did not have time to find him. He would have to manage by himself.

Accordingly, after Annia had left, he waited a short time, then going into the garden, walked past the pond to the garden door. Before he got there he began to feel extremely tired. Suddenly he found he was face down by the pond. For some reason he had fallen over. He could not be drunk – he had only had one glass of wine. Must have fallen over something. He did feel sleepy – he wished he didn't have to follow Annia, he would much rather go to bed. He struggled to his feet only to fall into an oleander bush. As he lost consciousness he thought he heard Annia laugh …

CHAPTER SIX

Marcus was vaguely conscious of people talking, one seemed to be Stronnius. He remembered he was going somewhere but his body did not feel as if it belonged to him, in fact he didn't think he had a body. There was a blank period then he woke to discover that he did indeed have a body or at least a head which felt as if it was about to fall off. He groaned.

"Master? Are you awake?"

Marcus cautiously opened his eyes to find it was daylight and he was in the workroom, lying on what appeared to be sacks with Stronnius anxiously bending over him.

"What happened?"

"Aulus found you in the garden early this morning. We think you've been drugged."

"Drugged – of course not."

He made as if to get up.

"Do you think you should move, Master? Why not stay here for a while?"

"I can't stay here. Help me up."

"Better not go into the house yet, Master."

"Why not?"

But Stronnius had gone. Marcus lay back and closed his eyes – he would rest for a while then go and find out what all this was about. The next time he awoke the afternoon was far advanced and he cautiously rose to his feet. He was still slightly dizzy but, thank Apollo Medicus, his headache had nearly gone. Outside the usual busy activity of garden slaves was missing. Everything was very quiet. Where were they all? He made his way to the terrace where he was met by Stronnius.

"The Master is waiting for you in the library. He sent me to fetch you."

"The Senator is *here?* What has happened Stronnius – where are all the slaves?"

"The Master will explain everything."

As Stronnius hurried him through the Atrium to the library he noticed that there was not one house slave to be seen. Sextus was sitting at his desk, writing.

"There you are, Rutilius. You've been drugged so Stronnius tells me."

"I can't have been. By whom? Incidentally you must be wrong about Annia, she is as chaste as a Vestal Virgin!"

"Considering the laxity of the present incumbents I agree with you."

Marcus did not know what to make of this but plunged on.

"You got my reports?"

"Yes, I got your reports. Very interesting but totally inaccurate, of course."

Marcus was indignant.

"Inaccurate! How could they be! I had Annia in sight all day, every day. I walked every inch of Puteoli and Baeae after her and I can guarantee that she never spoke to anyone unless I was present – except last night, of course, when she went to visit some women."

"And you followed her? Which house? The name of the women?"

"Well, no, last night I couldn't because I was —"

"As I said – drugged. You have played your part very well, Rutilius, and you will not find me ungrateful. You look perplexed. I will enlighten you. I had already arranged for a professional investigator to be infiltrated into the household and—"

Marcus looked at Stronnius who shook his head.

"No, it was not Stronnius. By the way he told me how you went after him when he so foolishly ran away and I have decided to punish him by freeing him immediately so that he won't be tempted to run away again. I am going to put him in charge of the house and gardens. I intend to retire very soon. I no longer enjoy Rome and I want to spend my last years in comfort. As I was saying, I had a spy in the household – no I won't tell you who it is. He, quite rightly, insists on preserving his anonymity. Your reports were opened and read by Annia and Lucius—"

"Lucius!"

Now things that had puzzled him began to fall into place. No wonder Annia was so familiar with the slave!

"How you do interrupt – yes, Annia and Lucius. Lucius who made sure your wine was drugged every night – not the way to treat good Falernian wine. You knew every move she made during the day, they made sure of that, but what of the night, eh? That's where my man – let us call him 'X' – came in. He was quite amused at the lengths they went to to make sure you were kept busy following Annia during the day. I understand you nearly lost her several times at Puteoli but she made sure you picked up the trail again. He sent me regular reports and those reports were not tampered with. Each negative report you sent increased their feeling of security. When X sent me a coded signal informing me that they were becoming careless I set out from Rome immediately. I could not have planned it better. There *were* no women to visit and, as I expected, I caught Lucius and Annia in flagrante delicto and I found *you* in an oleander bush."

"Lucius!" Marcus repeated, stunned.

"And you had no idea at all?" Sextus asked, incredulously.

Marcus remembered the conversation he had overheard. It had been between Annia and Lucius. There was no wall-painter. He should have known. He had considered the possibility but, at the time, had dismissed it as ridiculous.

"No, none," he lied. "Lucius should be severely punished!"

"Quite. He had been in my service a long time but," Sextus's voice hardened, "once a slave has abused his position there is only one thing to do with him."

Marcus noticed the use of the past tense and thanked whichever god it was that gave him a strong sense of self-preservation otherwise he had no doubt he would have joined Lucius in the Underworld. Sextus watched the expressions chasing themselves over Marcus's face.

"You played your part well. I had to make sure they thought they were in control of the situation. Had any of your reports revealed your knowledge of the true state of affairs I can assure you you would have been disposed of. Don't forget Annia has killed before. She would not think twice about it and Lucius would have helped her. Consider what was at stake."

"And Annia?"

"She decided to commit suicide."

He could not imagine Annia doing any such thing. How dare Sextus use him, well he would use Sextus.

"Of course she did although some people might wonder, if they found out of course, why somebody like Annia would commit suicide. Would make quite a scandal in Rome I should think. Might make things difficult for you if the facts became known."

Marcus heard Stronnius draw a sharp breath.

The Senator's face went white with fury.

"Do not threaten me, Rutilius, or it will be the worse for you. And I can assure you that any family connections you may think you have will not save you."

"But you used me!"

"Of course. When you appeared so providentially in Rome I knew I could use you to find out the truth."

Marcus rounded on Stronnius.

"Did you know what was going on?"

"No, I didn't but even if I had known I would not have told you. My loyalty is to my Master".

Marcus realized he had made a bad mistake. He made haste to reassure the Senator.

"I understand now, Senator. Of course your secret is safe with me. You misunderstood me. I only meant—"

Sextus held up his hand for silence opened a drawer in his desk, removed a money bag together with a scroll and placed both on the desk saying.

"This is for your trouble. Here is enough money and to spare to set you up in Rome in any profession you fancy but I shouldn't try spying if I were you. I don't think you're very good at it. Also a letter to Pharnaces, Captain of my merchant ship the Isis of Geminus which is moored at Puteoli. I have given the Captain instructions to take you back to Rome. You will probably find him in a tavern. You can have the litter to take you to the harbour."

With a dismissive gesture Sextus took up a stylus.

Picking up the bag and scroll, Marcus turned to go and then hesitated.

Irritated Sextus looked up

"Well, what is it?"

"I would rather not take the litter if you don't mind."

"Squeamish are you – very well, Stronnius will take you in the cart tomorrow. Farewell, a safe voyage. We shall not meet again unless you decide to ignore my warning but I don't think you will."

Sextus began to write. He did not look up as Marcus and Stronnius left the library.

Any hope that Marcus might still have cherished that Sextus would become his patron, died.

Marcus went along to the bath suite to find it deserted and cold. He ate a solitary dinner waited on by Stronnius.

"Stronnius, what has happened to the slaves – are they—?"

"No, no of course not. The Master is not a monster. He knew they were terrified of Lucius and does not blame them for keeping quiet. They and the garden slaves are in the slaves' quarters celebrating. There is nothing like a celebration for making up differences."

"When you are free will you go back to Gaul and search for your family?"

"Not immediately. I will see to everything here first. My Mast… Sextus Gaius Quintilius has promised me he will do everything he can to help me get back to Gaul and find them. He warned me that they are probably dead but I must know for certain. Once I have done that I shall come back and stay with the Senator as long as he needs me."

Marcus left the Villa the next day without a backward glance.

An excited Aulus drove them to Puteoli. He did not bother to conceal the fact that he was overjoyed by Lucius's downfall.

"You'll have to be careful now that Stronnius is to be freed." Marcus teased him.

Before Aulus could reply Stronnius said, "I'm going to ask the Senator if I can have Aulus as my personal slave."

"I hope you will take me to Gaul with you, Master. I have never been to Gaul," Aulus grinned.

"Don't call me Master, Aulus. You'll come to Gaul with me and when we come back I'll free you."

Aulus became very agitated. Marcus thought it was due to excitement at the prospect of being free for the first time in his life but he was wrong. Turning an anguished face to Stronnius, Aulus pleaded.

"Oh please don't free me! I don't want to be free! I've always been a slave. I couldn't live as a freeman."

"Very well, Aulus," Stronnius said, kindly. "I'll not mention it again unless you mention it first."

By mutual consent they all became very merry and the journey seemed no sooner to have begun than it ended at the quayside.

"I expect the Captain is in the quayside tavern. He doesn't like to be too far from his ship."

Marcus was quite sorry to be leaving them but, as he reminded himself, he was on his way back to Rome with full pockets. He could pay off his debts – he would have to think up some reason for his miraculous return from the dead – memory loss due to being buried alive perhaps. He had the whole voyage to think out the details.

Going into the tavern Stronnius had indicated he pushed his way through the crowd to the counter where he asked the slave dispensing drinks where he might find Captain Pharnaces. The slave waved a filthy hand at a table in the corner where a small, thickset man was sitting gazing into an empty wine glass.

"Captain Pharnaces?"

The man looked up. He did not smile.

"Who wants to know?" He growled.

"Marcus Rutilius. I have a letter from Senator Sextus Caius Quintilius"

Marcus replied, crisply.

Captain Pharnaces took the scroll and proceeded to read, mouthing the words half aloud. At one point he looked sharply at Marcus then went on reading to the end. He then carefully put the scroll away in a pouch at his belt.

"Thirsty work – reading." he remarked, thoughtfully.

Sitting down at the table, Marcus beckoned to the slave and ordered two glasses of Sabine wine.

He watched as the Captain buried his face in his glass not surfacing until it was empty. He looked at Marcus who stared back. Finally, realizing that there were no more drinks coming from that quarter and, wiping his mouth on the back of his hand, Pharnaces stated

"The Senator tells me you did him a service and that I am to take you to Rome. He does not say what the service was?"

Marcus remaining silent, he went on, "I will have to charge you, of course. Normally we don't carry passengers which makes it a special journey."

"The Senator gave *me* to understand that I would have a *free* passage back to Rome."

"Alright, alright," Pharnaces said, holding up his hands, "but you must agree you need to eat – the Senator only ordered me to give you passage back to Rome – he said nothing about providing your food."

Marcus realized that the Captain was as cunning as a Barbarian and would need watching.

"And how much would that be?" Marcus asked, coldly.

"Well . . ."

He looked Marcus up and down obviously calculating how much he could afford to charge him.

"Say 200 sesterces – in advance."

"200!" Marcus was outraged.

"Well, 150 then. As you're the only passenger you'll be getting Tribune treatment."

Marcus forbore to point out that Pharnaces had said he did not usually take passengers.

Very grudgingly Marcus counted out 150 sesterces.

"I shall expect *decent* food for this – do you understand?"

Pharnaces, carefully counting the money, ignored the comment. After he had safely stowed the money in his money pouch he asked.

"Tell me where you're staying. I'll send one of the crew for you when we're ready to sail. It should be before midnight if we are to catch the tide. If the weather is fair we should arrive at Rome in three days."

Marcus had no intention of letting the Captain out of his sight until he was safely on board The Isis of Geminus.

"I'll come with you and stay on the ship until it sails."

Pharnaces did not look pleased and Marcus's suspicions deepened.

"Don't you want to say goodbye to somebody? Friend, Mother, wife, girlfriend?"

"No"

"Somebody waiting for you in Rome, perhaps?"

"NO! What does it matter?"

Marcus was getting angry. Pharnaces shrugged and rose to his feet.

"Best be getting back on board then."

They left the tavern and in a few moments were at the quayside which was busy with ships loading and unloading, slaves carrying loads up and down gangways and overseers shouting orders. Everything looked in confusion. Pharnaces, however, seemed to know where he was going and, dodging in and out of the crowd, led the way. Finally the Captain stopped beside a ship which, Marcus was dismayed to note, was much smaller than he had thought it would be.

"This is it – The Isis of Geminus, the best ship on Our Sea."

Pharnaces was clearly extremely proud of his command. Marcus noticed how smart it looked compared to its Captain. It had a round, tubby hull, with one mast amidships. The stem was decorated with an elegantly carved swan's neck and head. On deck two men and a boy were bustling about with ropes. Watching the crew at work was a tall, thin man who was standing on the top of the deckhouse which afforded him an uninterrupted view of the whole deck.

Pharnaces strode up the gangway. Once on deck he bellowed, "Publius!"

The thin man clattered down to the deck.

"Captain?"

"Publius, this is Marcus who is sailing with us as a special passenger. He will sleep in the cabin. You can sleep on deck with the crew."

With displeasure, Marcus noted Pharnaces' use of the familiar form of address.

Publius nodded in agreement but did not look very pleased with the arrangement.

Leaning over the rail, Pharnaces shouted down to the deck, "Here you, boy!"

The boy, busy coiling a rope, looked up

"Yesser?"

"Take the passenger below and look sharp."

The boy led Marcus to a door in the deckhouse which opened onto a surprisingly commodius cabin containing two wooden box beds with blankets neatly folded at the foot of each. Upon inspection Marcus was pleased to find that the blankets appeared to be clean and free of vermin. The mattress however was very thin. Well, he had slept on thin mattresses before. He turned to the boy.

"When do we sail?"

"I heard the Captain tell Publius that he wants to be away soon."

Marcus vaguely remembered various rituals that he had watched in Rome before a ship sailed.

"After he has sacrificed to Isis I suppose?"

"Oh no, the Captain doesn't bother with all that, he even sails at the end of the month! He says" giving a passing imitation of Pharnaces's rasping voice "'if other Captains are stupid enough to throw away good cargoes, I'm not!'"

It was clear that, in his eyes at least Pharnaces was a hero. Reverting to his own voice he continued, importantly, "I must get back on deck. It's my job to hoist the basket – we can't sail until I've done that."

"Basket? What basket?"

The boy looked at him as if he could not believe anyone could be so stupid.

"The basket to show we're a merchant ship of course!"

The last words were shouted as he ran out on deck.

Thankfully, Marcus lay down on one of the beds. He was very tired in spite of the heavy sleep he had had the night before. He thought he might go out on deck and see the last of Puteoli before they sailed, but was fast asleep before he could summon up the energy to get off the bed.

CHAPTER SEVEN

Marcus was awakened by a great deal of noise, shouting and stamping of feet. Going to the deckhouse door he looked along the deck to see a red-faced Pharnaces confronting a large Centurion flanked by two soldiers. They had evidently just arrived at the top of the gangway.

"This is a merchant ship not a galley in case you haven't noticed."

Pharnaces shouted, waving his hand at the basket hanging from the stern.

"Can't help that, I have the authority to commandeer this ship and crew if necessary."

"Why this ship and on whose authority?"

"I need a small, fast ship. This is the smallest and looks reasonably fast. As for authority you have heard of Gaius Julius Caesar I suppose?"

The centurion was heavily sarcastic.

"The Senator Sextus Caius Quintilius owns this ship. Have you asked him if you can take it?"

"Don't need to. All I need do is to come on board, declare that I am commandeering the ship in an emergency and there is nothing you can do about it."

"I don't believe you can do that. I never heard of such a thing when I was in the Army. And I did my time."

The Centurion peered at Pharnaces

"You were in the Army were you – which legion?"

"The best in the Army – the VIIth."

The Centurion mellowed.

"Of course it's the best, it's *my* legion."

Turning to the two soldiers he ordered, "You two, make sure the crew don't make a run for it."

To Pharnaces he remarked, "Hot isn't it. Got anything to drink?"

As Pharnaces and the Centurion moved towards the deckhouse Marcus hastily moved back from the doorway. He realized that, coming as they did from the light of the deck into the comparative dark of the deckhouse, he could not be seen. Turning in the doorway Pharnaces shouted to the boy "Fetch wine!" As he got inside he announced, "Captain Pharnaces, retired Centurion."

"Centurion Decrius Marcellinus, lst Cohort, VIIth Legion. As you are one of us so to speak I can tell you the truth." Then he saw Marcus "Who's this?"

"A passenger I'm taking to Rome on Senator Sextus Caius Quintilius' orders."

Decrius looked hard at Marcus.

"Haven't I seen you before?"

"No, I don't think so."

"You remind me of someone – can't think who."

"Funny you should say that" Pharnaces remarked "I have had the same thought."

"What is your name?"

The Centurion sounded suspicious.

"Marcus Rutilius. Senator Sextus Caius Quintilius is my Patron."

Marcus told him, grandly – well, he nearly was.

To Marcus's relief this seemed to satisfy the Centurion. The boy appeared with a flagon of wine and Pharnaces poured out three glasses.

Taking a glass Decrius sat down on one of the beds carefully depositing his helmet and wand of office by his side.

"Well, its like this. My tribune, Domitius Proclus, is very keen to get into Caesar's good books which he won't because Caesar hates tribunes. Caesar is getting together a fleet at Portus Itius, something about an invasion. The ships he ordered were not up to scratch. Someone had been cutting too many corners, as usual. Caesar flew into one of his rages and had the builders flogged – should've crucified them if you ask me – anyway, now he was several ships short. Proclus goes to see Caesar and says that he will get some ships. Didn't think how he was going to do it, of course."

"Tribunes can't think!" Pharnaces remarked.

Nodding in agreement the Centurion continued.

"Caesar is a bit sceptical but Proclus insists that he can do it. Afterwards, when our clever Tribune has time to think about it he realizes that he hasn't the least idea how he is going to get any ships so, of course, he comes to me."

Shaking his head the Captain poured himself another drink.

"Knowing that there are usually plenty of ships here at Puteoli – I have a girl I visit here – I suggest that he commandeers a couple. So Proclus takes one of the ships from Portus Itius and we sail here. Proclus does his stuff and commandeers the ships – I had to tell him which ones, of course – need nursemaids these Tribunes – he feels tired as he was seasick all the way here so decides that he will have a rest before we start back so I take the opportunity to go and see my girl, taking two of the men with me (she has several sisters). We had a very good night, too good in fact because we didn't surface until this morning. When we came down to the quay we found the ships we commandeered plus the one we came in gone, so we were stuck until I had the idea of commandeering a fast ship to take us back to Portus Itius."

The Centurion took a hearty swig from his glass.

Pharnaces looked thoughtful.

"To Portus Itius. That should only take a few days. It will make a change from going from here to Rome and back. I've missed the excitement of the army. Sextus can't object if we tell him that we have been commandeered. You must give me some documentation – something about doing Caesar a favour or something."

"I can do that. One of the men writes a good hand."

Marcus spoke at last.

"You were ordered to take me to Rome, not Portus Itius."

Pharnaces snorted impatiently, "I can take you to Rome once we have put the Centurion here ashore. You'll only lose a few days, and what's a few days? And you said yourself there is nobody waiting for you."

Marcus could think of no valid reason to insist on going to Rome and the Centurion was rather large – he also had the authority of the Army behind him.

"Yes, I suppose I can wait."

"Good – that's settled. Now I must get us under way or we'll miss the tide."

Flinging himself back on the bed, the Centurion was soon snoring. Marcus lay down on the other and tried to get back to sleep but it took a long time and there was still no sign of food, but that didn't matter as he had somehow stopped feeling hungry.

Marcus found the next few days extremely miserable as, unlike the smooth sea at Baeae, this sea was rough. He had not known that a ship could move so much and in so many directions at once. He was seasick almost as soon as they were under way spending most of his time on deck. Dying would have been a relief. The Centurion seemed to have taken up residence in the deckhouse.

Part of the cargo was amphorae of wine and the boy, who didn't seem to have any other name, was kept busy fetching wine for Decrius and Pharnaces who kept the Centurion company talking over old battles which Marcus found boring but the worst thing was when Decrius insisted on reliving, in graphic detail, every battle he had taken part in together with how he acquired his wounds. This did not help Marcus to feel any better and he spent more and more time hanging over the side of the ship wishing the journey would end. One night, he was woken from a fitful sleep by the sound of Pharnaces and Decrius singing. The song seemed to have innumerable verses and they bellowed out the chorus after each verse:

"Home we bring our bald whoremonger;
Romans, lock your wives away!
All the bags of gold you lent him
Went his Gallic tarts to pay."

Groaning, he wrapped his cape tighter round himself pulling the hood over his head to try and cut out the noise.

During the night he was conscious of somebody standing over him saying urgently, "Rutilius, Rutilius, wake up!"

It was the Centurion and one of the soldiers.

Marcus groaned, "Listen, Rutilius, this is important"

Decimus pulled his hood away from his head.

"I am leaving Livius with you. He is very trustworthy. He will look after you and make sure you don't fall overboard."

Marcus wished everyone would leave him alone. Decrius seemed to expect an answer so he grunted. To his relief this seemed to satisfy the Centurion who nodded and walked away. Marcus settled back to sleep.

As time went on Marcus began to feel better but not safe enough to leave the deck.

Everyone ignored him except Livius. The other soldier, whom Livius addressed as Fabius, thought all this solicitude on Livius's part totally unnecessary.

"Leave him, Livius. He's only a civilian!"

"Decrius told me to look after him."

"Why, what's so special about him?"

"I don't know but Decrius seems to think there is something. Anyway, it's nothing to do with you."

"Well, if you want to be nursemaid to some seasick civilian its up to you. I'm off for my dinner. Hope it's not greasy pork again."

He added, maliciously, watching Marcus who groaned and crawled to the ship's side. Later, Livius tried to get Marcus to eat some boiled fish and drink some sips of wine. To Fabius's obvious disgust he continued to look after Marcus and at night he covered him with his own cloak. Sometimes he talked about his home. He came from a farming family and missed them very much.

"Still, my 25 years will be over one day and then I shall go back home and never leave. If I don't get killed, that is."

One night Marcus lay, as usual, at the foot of the mast where the ship didn't appear to move quite so much trying to get some sleep. He was just dozing off when he felt hands at his waist, realizing that someone was trying to get his money pouch from his belt, he cried out and Livius who had been sleeping nearby appeared sword in hand. Livius grabbed Publius by the back of his tunic at the same time pressing the point of his sword painfully into his back.

"You will leave Rutilius alone unless you want to feel a few more inches of this sword" he told him.

Publius seemed inclined to argue.

"Mind your own business, Legionary. Why is he so special?"

"Were you in the Army?" Livius asked.

"I did my time – same Legion as Pharnaces. Why do you want to know?"

Instead of answering Livius ordered.

"Get a lamp and look at him – carefully."

Publius opened his mouth to say something but changed his mind when he felt a prod from Livius's sword. Grumbling he went and fetched a lamp which he held so that the light fell full on Marcus's face who blinked, blinded by the glare.

Grasping Publius's tunic Livius bent him close to Marcus's face.

"Look at him! Who does he look like?"

Publius peered at Marcus then stepped back in spite of the sword in his back.

"By all the gods – Caesar!"

"So, take very great care you don't upset him or you could regret it."

Fabius appeared from out of the darkness and briefly peered at Marcus.

"He doesn't look anything like Caesar to me. Now, can we get some sleep!"

Irritably pulling his cloak tighter round himself he stomped back to his sleeping place on deck.

Still keeping a grip on Publius, Livius told him, "Remember what I said."

He let him go. Muttering imprecations Publius stumbled off into the darkness.

In spite of Fabius's derogatory remarks Marcus felt a surge of exultation. That was why people sometimes stared at him in the street! Why Sextus had been so startled when he saw him after he was cleaned up. And, yes, why Julia would never tell him who his father was. He must see Caesar as soon as he could – Caesar would not be able to acknowledge him openly – he had too many enemies but he would surely do something for him. He always *knew* he was the son of somebody important! What was it the Sibyl had said? Something about 'one day becoming a great man'? Obviously, Caesar's son *would* be a great man! Livius was saying something.

"Decrius ordered me to keep an eye on you. I don't think he trusts Pharnaces. He also realized who you reminded him of. Like the rest of the Army he admires Caesar so is not likely to let anything happen to a close relative of his Commander. You can tell me, are you . . .?"

"I don't know. I have never seen Caesar up close."

"Well I have and I can tell you you look like a young Caesar but whether you are or not makes no difference. It could work to your advantage – look at the effect it had on Publius."

Marcus said nothing for a while then, "It could be useful I suppose."

"Try and get back to sleep now. I don't think you will have any more trouble from Publius or anyone else but I will be here on guard."

As Marcus lay back against the mast, Livius tucked his cloak round him and left him to sleep.

All the passengers and crew were on deck as they came into Portus Itius. Everyone kept their distance from Pharnaces who was suffering a hangover and, consequently, extremely bad tempered. Decrius, on the other hand, seemed as fresh as when he first appeared at the top of the gangway at Puteoli.

As The Isis came into the harbour Fabius exclaimed, "Look at that!"

Marcus was speechless. The harbour was jammed with ships most of them dwarfing The Isis. Everywhere was activity as the Army prepared to embark.

"I have never seen anything like it," Livius exclaimed.

"The Britons will surrender as soon as they see this fleet."

Decrius said with satisfaction. He motioned to Marcus.

"A word with you."

As the Centurion led Marcus away from the others Pharnaces and Publius stopped talking and watched them. Decrius turned his back on the Captain and gestured for Marcus to do the same. Lowering his voice he said, "Pharnaces has decided to go over to Britain. From what he said I think he intends to fake the sinking of The Isis, change the name and go into business on his own account."

Looking round at Pharnaces, Decrius pulled Marcus further along the deck, lowering his voice still further he said, "Pharnaces got very drunk and boasted that he was going to be very rich. 'How is that?' I asked. "Apparently, Sextus, who sounds a good man but too trusting – surprising in a Senator – likes to help people when he can and has sent quite a few to Pharnaces over the years to give them free passage either to Puteoli or Rome. Pharnaces finds out if they have anyone likely to miss them and if, like you, they are alone in the world he orders Publius to drop them over the side after robbing them, then they split the money between them.

Don't look round! Why do you think I ordered Livius to guard you? I had been trying to think who you reminded me of and then it came to me – Caesar! Now, normally I wouldn't interfere in a civilian matter but I was not going to stand by while our Caesar's son – yes, you must be, – was murdered! Pharnaces is a disgrace to the Eagle of the VIIth. If he was under my command he would wish he had never been born! If Livius had not been so alert you would be feeding the fishes by now!"

"Thank you for everything, Decrius. I am most grateful."

"Well, you take care. I don't think Pharnaces will harm you now but be alert."

He strode to the top of the gangway which was being put into place.

"Livius! Flavius!"

Livius, after making a quick gesture of farewell to Marcus, fell in with Flavius behind Decrius.The Centurion shouted, "MARCH!"

Keeping in perfect step they all three marched smartly down the gangway and off the ship.

As Marcus watched them out of sight there was a sudden flurry along the quayside. Soldiers stopped what they were doing and put down their burdens.They all seemed to be looking in one direction. Marcus craned his neck but found it difficult to see past the large trireme moored next to and dwarfing The Isis.

Publius appeared at his side.

"What did Decrius say to you?"

"He was trying to get me to join the Army."

"And will you?"

Before Marcus could think of a suitable reply Pharnaces, leaning excitedly over the rail called out, "I do believe it's Caesar! Look."

An imposing figure, tall, fair-haired and bare-headed, Caesar strode down the quay, his aides having difficulty keeping up with him. By Marcus's side Pharnaces had gone to the salute and the rest of the crew were hanging over the ship's side craning their necks.

They watched as Caesar, arriving at the trireme next to The Isis, made to go on board. At the foot of the gangway he paused to speak to an aide and glanced over at The Isis. Marcus looked at the Commander. The thought ran through Marcus's mind – could this be the face of his father? They seemed to look at each other for hours but it could only have been seconds then Caesar turned and walked up the gangway.

Marcus was disappointed at Caesar's lack of reaction but consoled himself with the thought that the Commander probably thought it best for them not to call attention to themselves.

Pharnaces relaxed.

"Caesar remembered me! Did you see the way he looked at me? He never forgets a man who has served under him. I am going to go and offer The Isis as a transport ship. Publius – I am going aboard that trireme to speak to Caesar!"

"You can't just go and demand to speak to him." Marcus was shocked.

"Oh yes, I can. Caesar is always available to the humblest soldier."

"You're not a . . ."

But Pharnaces was already striding down the gangway.

The Captain was away for a long time and Marcus became bored waiting. Publius settled down on a coil of rope and went to sleep, the rest of the crew following his example.

Marcus had just decided to go ashore when he saw Pharnaces, and a Centurion heading a column of soldiers marching down the quay. He looked to see if Livius was amongst them but they were all strangers.

The moment Pharnaces's foot touched the bottom of the gangway Publius sprang up from a deep sleep as if by magic and kicked the rest of the crew into life.

The Captain strode on board as if The Isis had suddenly become a three-oared trireme.

"Find quarters for these men." he ordered.

"Can I have a word with you, Marcus Rutilius?"

Marcus noticed the formal use of his name.

"Certainly" he replied and waited for Pharnaces to come to him.

"Yes, what is it?"

"I'm sorry about that misunderstanding with Publius. It was not until I saw Caesar that I realized who you resembled."

Forgetting to be on his dignity Marcus eagerly asked

"Did Caesar say anything about me?"

"He asked me how many crew I had and who you were."

"And then? What did he say then?"

"He accepted The Isis as a transport and then he ordered me to make sure you came with us to Britain."

"Why?"

"I don't know! Who knows what Caesar is thinking? The only thing you can be sure of is that he never says anything without a reason. He did tell me not to start making assumptions and if he heard any rumours about his private life he would be most displeased. Then he called Titus Atticus Labienus, his Second in Command, and ordered him to assign us our men, then he dismissed me and here I am."

Marcus was disappointed. Then he brightened – perhaps Caesar intended sending for him once they were in Britain. Everyone said that the Britons would welcome Caesar with open arms. Once the Commander was comfortably settled he would speak to him. Perhaps he would acknowledge him as his son! Marcus lost himself in a very pleasant daydream of his life as Caesar's son. He came back to reality to hear Pharnaces saying, "...so we sail at midnight."

During an evening meal of fresh fish, fruit and a flagon of wine Marcus was afraid he would have to put up with Pharnaces and the Centurion going over yet more battles but mercifully the Centurion was a member of the Xth Legion. Pharnaces being a civilian and an ex-VIIth the Centurion was civil but distant. Pharnaces, saying that he had to get some sleep as he would be at his post on deck all night, left them finishing their meal. Marcus and the Centurion retired soon afterwards. Unlike Decrius the Centurion did not snore. Some time later Marcus woke and was delighted to realize that the movement did not worry him in the least. The cabin felt hot and stuffy and his head ached so he decided to go up on deck for some fresh air. As he reached the deck he felt a soft, refreshing breeze on his face. Climbing the ladder to the upper deck, he found Pharnaces and the rest of the crew keeping lookout. Pharnaces beckoned to him saying

"Look at that – you'll never see anything like that again."

Marcus looked. As far as he could see in any direction were gently bobbing lights. The Isis was completely surrounded by ships and every ship had at least one lamp. It was a calm, clear night. He found it eerie, stars above them the points of light reflected in the sea, giving the impression that the ships were suspended between sky and sea. He stayed on deck for a long time, reluctant to go back to the darkness of the cabin. Eventually, when fatigue caught up with him, he made his way back to bed and propped the door open so that he could look out and watch the stars and the lamps until he fell asleep.

CHAPTER EIGHT

The next time Marcus woke it was daylight and the Centurion's bed was empty. Hastily getting up he went out on deck. The sea ahead and on either side was covered with large and small ships but, no matter what the size, they each had at least one small boat attached which bobbed along behind. Astern, the sea was empty. They must be in the rear of the fleet. Turning back he saw that the ships ahead were converging on what appeared to be a large white cloud. Pharnaces and Publius were also peering ahead at the cloud.

"What is *that!*" Marcus asked.

Pharnaces turned.

"That is Britain – the edge of the world. The land of the dead."

"Why do you call it the land of the dead?"

Marcus asked with a shiver that was not entirely due to the cool air off the sea.

"I have seen things."

"Things?"

"Fishing boats – with no crew – sailing on their own – it is said that they carry the souls of the dead to Britain. That's why people call it the land of the dead. It's a very nasty place, there are reptiles hundreds of feet long and places where no man can live because of the poisonous air. Most of the time it's shrouded in mist in order to keep its secrets."

Pharnaces' voice had sunk to a whisper by the time he finished speaking.

"Why go then?" Marcus asked.

"Because our Commander tells us to. Now you, Captain, get on with your duties and you, sailor, keep a proper lookout – if we run into the ship in front I'll have you crucified!"

The Centurion sounded as if he meant it. Pharnaces glowered at the Centurion who gazed back at him impassively. Pharnaces made as if to speak but changing his mind walked away. Turning to Marcus the Centurion said, "Don't believe everything you hear, Marcus Rutilius."

"You know my name?"

"Oh yes, Decrius Marcellinus told me about you."

Marcus was on the point of asking what had been said about him when the Centurion pointed at the cliffs and shouted, "Look there!"

The others had seen it at the same time – the cliff tops were full of men. The ships ahead began to slow. There was the sound of anchors being lowered. Pharnaces came and stood by Marcus and the Centurion.

"They don't look very friendly. I thought we were going to be welcomed?" Marcus said, puzzled.

"Well, it doesn't look like it," Pharnaces replied.

"They've got *chariots* up there!" The Centurion sounded astonished.

"Chariots? I've never seen them outside the arena."

Marcus peered upwards.

"Of course you haven't," The Centurion replied, impatiently.

"We only use them for racing but these Barbarians seem to use them as *war* chariots!"

He sounded scornful, and added, "It will make no difference, they won't stand a chance against our Army!"

A small boat detached itself from the ship in front and headed for The Isis. Going to the side of the ship Pharnaces peered down at the men in the boat. After some shouted conversation he came back to where they all waited. The small boat rowed off busily to the next ship.

"Looks as if you're wanted, Centurion."

The Centurion grunted and called one of the soldiers.

"Caesius Scaeva!"

A soldier approached his Centurion, saluted and waited for orders.

"I have to go to the Command ship. You are now in charge. Await my return."

While the Centurion was giving his orders, Pharnaces called the boy to him and ordered him to take the Centurion to Caesar's warship.

Settling his helmet firmly on his head, the Centurion descended the rope ladder to the boat where the boy was waiting.

Marcus watched as the boy skilfully steered his way between the anchored ships.

"Why don't we land?" he asked Pharnaces.

"Look at those cliffs. See how sheer they are? If the Britons *are* unfriendly, and they certainly look it to me, they can easily fire down on us and pick us off with no trouble. I expect Caesar has called a conference. We just have to wait for his orders."

Pharnaces sounded very cheerful about it.

As soon as the boy came back Pharnaces told him to prepare something to eat.

"Never know when you'll get a chance to eat when you're on campaign so we'll eat while we can."

Marcus was not feeling particularly hungry but made an effort. He didn't want Pharnaces, who ate as if he was in his favourite tavern in Puteoli, to know how frightened he was. It was the waiting he found difficult. He had thought they would land to be met by Britons eager to welcome them, after all they *were* Romans, but these Britons seemed to have no idea of how to behave. It looked as if they were prepared to take on the most disciplined Army in the entire world, which could easily defeat them, Marcus reminded himself and instantly felt better.

They had only just finished their meal when Caesius Scaeva, a small, dark, thick-set man with no neck to speak of, pointed out their Centurion approaching in a small boat. Pharnaces waited impatiently for him to arrive on deck.

"Well?"

"Caesar is on the move to a better landing place. Keep an eye on that galley in front for signals."

He turned to the waiting solders.

"We are to stay on The Isis until ordered otherwise."

Marcus watched, fascinated, as the whole fleet raised anchor in unison and swung away from the shore to make its way slowly down the coast.

"They're still with us."

Pharnaces pointed out the Britons keeping pace with them along the top of the cliffs.

Another signal and the fleet swung shorewards.

"This looks a better landing place. The Britons will have to fight down on the beach now," Publius said with satisfaction.

They watched as the troop carriers were deployed in a line facing the beach.

"Why have they stopped?" Marcus enquired.

"Unfortunately it's low tide, don't think Caesar realized how much difference there is between this sea and Our Sea. The ships would run aground if they went any further in."

As the soldiers began to jump from the transports the Britons charged down the beach in chariots, on horseback, and on foot.

Marcus watched in dismay as the Romans, encumbered with armour and weapons, struggling to retain their footing in the swirling waves, sank to their chins in the water. The Britons, screaming blood-curdling war cries, raced into the waves hurling spears and whirling enormous swords round their heads. They were enough to frighten even the most hardened soldier – almost completely naked as they were and, incredibly, tattooed with bright blue swirls. Two-man war chariots, one man steering the horses the other man preparing to fight, were driven at speed into the water. The charioteers anticipating every move of their warriors swinging away before the Romans could get at them although here and there a horse would be wounded or the charioteer wounded or killed. On both sides wounded men were falling into the water and drowning.

"Now you'll see something to tell your grandchildren."

Pharnaces had seen another signal. The large warships suddenly backed then, the oars going so fast they were a blur, ran ashore and began throwing everything they had at the Britons on the beach, arrows, javelins, stones but the most spectacular sight were the heavy javelins being hurled as if they were twigs from large wooden catapulta mounted in the front of the galleys.

"Why have they done that?"

Marcus was thunderstruck.

"Wait," Pharnaces said impatiently, "see, the enemy are frightened out of their wits and so they should be. Now our soldiers will attack."

Marcus could feel the excitement beginning to mount. Pharnaces was almost beside himself. He kept repeating

"If *only* I could be there!"

The soldiers were equally excited and the boy was jumping up and down. The noise was tremendous.

Nothing happened, the Britons began to advance again and Pharnaces was nearly in tears.

"What are they waiting for? ATTACK!"

There was a flurry on one of the transports – a soldier suddenly appeared standing on the side of the boat holding aloft something that flashed in the sun.

"The standard of the Xth Legion," Pharnaces said.

The man was shouting something. All on board The Isis craned forward to hear what he was saying but could only hear snatches above the noise of the battle.

"Jump…comrades…want to surrender…eagle…I…do my duty …country…general."

Then he jumped into the water.

Everyone on The Isis cheered as men began to leap out of the transports and into the water.

"May Jupiter Maximus Optimus protect the eagle of the Xth!" one shouted.

But the Britons had recovered from their fright. As the Romans began to come ashore in ones and twos the Britons surrounded any isolated man as he set foot on shore, killed him and immediately looked for another victim to attack. Although the Romans fought fiercely and had superior weapons, they were no match for four or five Britons at once. All they could do was try and inflict as much damage as they could before they were killed. Soon the dead on both sides began to litter the shore. The combatants were standing on each other's dead and wounded to fight one another. All along the beach such Romans as had survived were running to the nearest standard.

"Look! Look!"

This time the sharp eyes of the boy had seen the signal.

Pharnaces absent-mindedly cuffed him and then read the signal.

"Right, time to use the boats."

Before he could give the order Publius had leaped into the small boat and at the same time the Centurion, calling his men to follow him, jumped down into the boat from the deck. For a moment it looked as if it would capsize but Publius steadied it. All over the sea men from other ships were leaping into the small boats. They rowed like fury to help any soldiers in trouble so that the Britons found they were no longer dealing with isolated men. Marcus watched as one boat capsized taking the men with it.

"What is that fool Publius doing?" Pharnaces shouted.

Marcus had a job to pick out their boat amidst all the others but then recognized Publius's tall frame in a boat which was steering straight for a flat-topped rock close to shore. Publius manoeuvred the boat to the rock and the men, jumping from the boat to the rock, began throwing their javelins at a group of Britons about to despatch a struggling Roman who had just managed to reach the beach. The Britons left the soldier who, unharmed, ran up the beach to one of the standards.

"Move, Move!"

The boy and Pharnaces shouted in unison.

They watched in horror as the water, which had been lapping round the rock, receded in the ebb. The Britons, seizing their chance, rushed across the uncovered beach whirling their swords. Publius rowed close to the rock and held on. The Centurion fell, an arrow through his thigh. Publius was gesturing to the men to get into the boat. Four of them picked up the wounded man, turned, and carried him along the rock to the boat. One man stayed with the clear intention of holding off the Britons while his comrades got away.

"Caesius Scaeva – get in the boat!"

Pharnaces shouted, forgetting in his excitement that there was no way he could be heard.

Caesius Scaeva threw his last javelin at the foremost Briton who fell, clutching his stomach. Turning on the others he put two more out of action with his sword thus gaining a few seconds respite then leaped into the water and swam towards the boat where he was pulled aboard by his comrades.

Turning the boat Publius began to row towards the nearest warship.

"Where is he going?"

Marcus had expected Publius to row back to The Isis.

"They must get the Centurion to the Medicus as soon as possible. Ah! – at last our soldiers are acting like Romans!"

Thanks to the frantic work of the little boats more and more men were forming into orderly ranks on the beach. One determined charge and the Britons were in full retreat. The Romans pursued them as fast as they could but, without the cavalry, were unable to catch them.

"Why is the cavalry late?" Pharnaces fumed – "and where is Publius? He should be back by now."

Pharnaces was restless until he saw Publius wearily rowing back alone. On reaching The Isis he threw a line to the boy and climbed up to where Pharnaces and Marcus were waiting.

"I've handed all the men over to the Medicus. Did you see Caesius Scaeva? You should see his face! He'll look a sight for a few days. The

Medicus asked me to hold the Centurion while he removed the arrow. It's a clean wound. Not like some we've seen, eh Pharnaces?"

He laughed and dug Pharnaces familiarly in the ribs.

Pharnaces gave him a withering look.

Undeterred Publius chattered on, "Caesius Scaeva was worried because he had lost his weapons and nothing we could say would cheer him up, he was convinced that he would be punished. WHAT IS THAT BOY DOING?"

He rushed off and buffeted the boy for no apparent reason.

Marcus went to bed, exhausted. He ached all over from tensing his muscles as he watched the landing and subsequent battle. He knew he would not sleep. His head was too full of images and speculation about what would happen now. He must have slept without realizing it as the next thing he knew it was broad daylight.

Yawning, Marcus made his way out on deck. Looking shorewards he could see that the warships had been hauled even further up the beach and hundreds of men were digging.

"What are they doing?" He asked Publius who was standing watching the activity on shore.

"Making camp. First thing you do in enemy territory. Let me show you" he said enthusiastically, pleased to have an audience. Taking out a bundle of note-tablets and a stylus from a pouch at his belt he began to draw.

"The camp is formed in a square like this. The warships will make one side between the camp and the sea in case the Britons decide to attack from that direction."

Marcus watched as Pharnaces sketched in a wide ditch, then a bank made from the earth.

"They will put sharpened stakes on top and then interweave it with branches – sharpened, of course."

"Of course." Marcus agreed.

Marcus paid close attention as the sketch took shape. He never lost an opportunity to gather information – it could be useful.

Pharnaces finished his sketch. A square camp. Each side of which had a bridge across the ditch and bank with a gate in the palisade.

"What are those?"

Marcus pointed at a section full of inverted "V's".

"The men's tents."

"And this one?"

Pointing at a larger "V" standing on its own.

"That's the Commander's tent and these," indicating more V's, "are the tents of the senior officers and the hospital tent."

"And they will build all that?"

"Oh yes. Each soldier has a section to dig, it will soon be done. Besides they are used to it. Probably done it hundreds of times."

Marcus glanced from the sketch to the camp site.

"Who are they?" he asked, indicating a line of horsemen making their way to the camp.

"It's the Britons, they've had enough. I told you we would conquer them – we usually do." Pharnaces said complacently.

Marcus found the next few days extremely boring. The only thing to watch was the camp taking shape and the comings and goings of the Britons. He wanted to go ashore but Pharnaces said he would only get in the way and was better off on board. They had visits from the crews of the other ships anchored all round them. But, as all they could talk about was the sea and its vagaries, Marcus left them to it.

By the fourth day the camp was complete. Pharnaces had taken the opportunity of cleaning the ship and kept the crew busy scrubbing and polishing. As the boy stood up and put his hand wearily to his back he glanced out to sea.

"Captain! Captain!" he called, excitedly.

"What is it?"

Pharnaces growled, looking to where the boy pointed.

Marcus also looked and saw a line of ships, he counted eighteen, sailing in line abreast.

"The cavalry – at last!" exclaimed Pharnaces.

"How soon will they get here?" Marcus asked

Pharnaces studied the sky, wet his finger and held it up "Before nightfall in this breeze." But Marcus noticed that he was frowning.

During the next two hours the breeze became stronger The Isis began to rock and Marcus refused his food.

Suddenly the sky became very dark and it began to rain heavily. Pharnaces shouted orders about anchors and securing ropes. Marcus hung onto anything he would reach and hoped. He could see nothing, the transports had disappeared in the murk. It became even darker as night fell. At the height of the storm and above the howling of the wind Marcus heard a sharp crack and grabbed the boy as he rushed past

"What has happened?" he shouted.

"The mast has gone," the boy shouted back and pulling himself out of Marcus's grasp was gone.

Several times during the long night Marcus thought they were going to sink. Pharnaces and Publius seemed to be everywhere at once.

The storm did not die down until dawn. In daylight he could see that everything was a shambles. The ships on either side of them were badly damaged, several ships further out to sea were rolling, their masts gone and their oars smashed to splinters. Men were throwing debris over the side. Looking round The Isis Marcus could see that, although the mast had snapped half way up and one anchor was gone, the other two that Pharnaces had prudently put out at the start of the storm still held and they were not so badly damaged as some of the other ships. He looked ashore to where the warships had been. There were sinister gaps and the sea was breaking over those remaining.

Pharnaces set them all to work clearing up the decks, even Marcus had to do his share of the work. They had just sent the boy to find out what unspoilt stores there were when they heard a hail from a small boat.

"Conference ashore for all the transport Captains" Pharnaces informed them.

Marcus had a feeling that Pharnaces was enjoying all this. The Captain was away for some time and when he returned he called them all together.

"Caesar is worried. Winter is coming on and we have no provisions for a prolonged stay on this barbaric island."

Marcus realized that, in his mind, Pharnaces had reverted to being a Centurion; he could almost see the uniform on him.

"The transports we saw have been scattered all over the sea. Probably gone back home so Caesar has decided to repair the least damaged ships, using material from the wrecked ones, in that way we can probably repair enough ships to get us home. Everyone must do their bit and that includes you, Rutilius, so I am putting you ashore – there is bound to be something you can do to help. Do you know Caesar even remembered my name? We are not going to let our Commander down. We don't have much time so you, boy, row Marcus ashore then get back here as quickly as possible."

"I'll get my things."

Marcus made to go to the cabin.

"No time." Pharnaces said, impatiently. "Anyway, you'll not be ashore for long."

"But..."

Pharnaces strode off. Marcus shrugged and followed the boy to the small boat which had once more been secured to The Isis's stern. The boat had survived but had sprung some leaks and Marcus was kept busy bailing out in order to keep them afloat.

When they reached shore the boy barely gave him time to disembark before rowing rapidly back to The Isis.

CHAPTER NINE

Once ashore, Marcus made his way to one of the camp entrances. Now he was close to it he could see the extent of the defensive ditch. He crossed via the wooden bridge to be met at the gate by a sentry who demanded to know who he was.

"I have been sent by Captain Pharnaces ofThe Isis of Geminus."

Not being satisfied with this answer, the sentry sent for his Centurion who, Marcus was delighted to discover, was none other than Decrius Marcellinus.

"Sent you ashore to help, have they?" Decrius sounded amused.

"Come with me."

As the Centurion led him through the camp Pharnace's sketch began to make sense.The camp was a square divided into two unequal rectangles bisected by a wide roadway which extended from one side of the camp to the other. Marcus was impressed by its size. He asked, as casually as he could, "Which is Caesar's tent?"

He intended speaking to the Commander as soon as possible to request that Pharnaces be ordered to take him back on boardThe Isis immediately.

Decrius pointed to the far end of the camp and, as if reading Marcus's mind, said, "Don't think about trying to see the Commander. You would never get past his bodyguard not to mentionTitus Atticus Labienus, Caesar's Second-in-Command."

Marcus said nothing but resolved to speak to Caesar all the same.

Decrius led the way to a large area divided into squares and covered with leather tents.As he stopped at one of the tents the soldier sitting outside sprang to his feet.

"You, Gaius Flaccus, look after this man. See that he has all he needs," Decrius ordered then, nodding to Marcus, he strode away.

The soldier relaxed.

"Who are you then?"

Evidently this Gaius Flaccus did not believe in beating about the bush.

"Marcus Rutilius."

"I thought I knew that voice."

When Livius came out of the tent Marcus was extremely pleased to see him, it was as well to be with someone who knew the ropes.

"Livius! Do you think Decrius put me with you deliberately?"

"Of course he did – that Centurion knows everything about everyone. He knows what you are thinking before you think it. This tent is only supposed to hold eight but you're in luck, Tettius was killed so you can have his place."

Gaius was evidently not particularly distressed at the death of his late comrade.

"Come from one of the ships have you?" Gaius enquired, looking him up and down.

Shooting Marcus a warning glance Livius answered for him.

"Yes, Rutilius is a member of a ship's crew. Sent by his Captain, I expect."

"Yes, that's right." Marcus agreed.

"You'll be used to hard work then."

Having satisfied himself on that point Gaius picked up his sword and began to clean it.

Saying he would give him some of the late Tettius's wardrobe, Livius took him inside the tent and warned him.

"Don't let the men know you're a civilian. They don't like civilians poking into their affairs. They like to keep things to themselves."

"What things?" Marcus asked, curiously.

"Oh, Army things. Nothing for you to worry about but be careful what you say, especially in front of Gaius, he can't keep anything to himself."

Marcus promised to be careful. Livius nodded and gave him several tunics and a leather waterproof cape.

Over the next few days Marcus got into the Army routine and took his turn with the other men of the VIIth, who alternated with the men of the Xth repairing ships one day and gathering corn the next. Marcus found it was not such a bad life and he ate regular meals. Although the other men in the tent were wary of him at first, being a friend of Livius who seemed to be popular, helped to ease his way and soon they relaxed and began treating him almost as one of themselves. At the day's end while they sat outside the tent playing dice, Marcus brought them up-to-date with the latest gossip from Rome. Most of the men had been away from home for many years so they listened eagerly. Marcus had wondered if the men would mention his resemblance to Caesar. They must have noticed it – they saw Caesar every day. Nothing was said and he concluded that Livius had warned them not to ask questions.

Marcus was enjoying himself and one day, finding himself alone with Livius, he asked his advice about joining the Army.

"I had a friend in Rome – Fabius Decimus who joined the Army. Perhaps you know him?"

Livius smiled and shook his head.

"The Army is very large, Rutilius."

"Well Fabius asked me to join with him. I wish I had now."

"My advice is to think carefully before you take the oath. Wait until you get back to Rome then make up your mind."

Upon reflection Marcus could see this was good advice. It would not be wise to sign on for years just on the strength of a few days.

On the day after this conversation it was the VIIth's turn to go out into the fields and gather corn. When Marcus asked Livius whose corn it was he shrugged and replied, "Who knows? The Roman Army takes what it wants."

All the corn in one field had already been cut and there was only the middle left in the other. They would soon have to look further afield. The men worked in pairs, Marcus and Livius working side by side and chatting as they scythed their way through the ripe corn. Livius liked to talk about his home and family.

"When I leave the Army I shall go home and never go away again. My parents are getting old and will be glad of help on the farm and, one day, who knows, I may even marry and raise some sons – none of whom will be allowed to join the Legion."

"Why did you join?" Marcus asked.

Livius did not answer, he was standing up and staring in the direction of the thick woods which grew up to one edge of the field.

"I thought I saw the sun glint on something. Perhaps we should arm ourselves."

Marcus stood and peered in the same direction but could see nothing. He looked round at the other men still working.

"It's nothing."

Marcus assured him. They bent back to their work. There was a sudden rushing sound and Livius was down on the ground, with a spear in his neck. Startled, Marcus stood up to see dozens of British chariots sweeping round the field. Spears and other missiles flew in all directions. Some of the men ran towards the stack of arms left in a corner of the field. Many fell and were run over by the wheels of the British chariots which were whirling round the field like lightning. A small group of Romans managed to get to their weapons and began fighting back. Marcus did the only thing he could think of – he lay down by Livius, smeared himself with some of his blood – of which there was plenty – and played dead.

When he heard some scattered cheering he cautiously raised his head. To his relief he saw the Britons retreating back into the woods as a column of Roman soldiers with Caesar himself at the head, drawn sword flashing in the sun, came to the rescue. As the men of the VIIth began making their way to the field edge Marcus ran up to one of them and clutched his arm.

"You must help me get Livius back to camp."

The soldier pulled back two of the men and the four of them returned to where Livius lay. The man took one look at Livius and shook his head. They carried Livius back to the camp hospital where the Medicus pronounced him dead.

"What about you, soldier?" he asked, looking at Marcus's bloodstained tunic. Marcus shook his head and left the hospital tent without replying.

The tent was very subdued that night. Gaius was nursing a wounded arm and was too busy worrying about the Medicus's warning that the arm might have to be amputated to be in any mood for speech. The rest of the men had wounds of varying degrees of severity. Marcus spent much of the night fetching water for the wounded and listening to their groans although he did find time just before dawn to change out of his blood-encrusted tunic. As he did so he heard the sound of rain on the sides of the leather tent.

It went on raining for days and days. Why, Marcus wondered wearily, would anyone want to conquer this damp piece of earth let alone live on it?

He was feeling extremely depressed. Nothing had prepared him for his first skirmish. Watching men die in the arena was one thing but being in the thick of it was quite another. He no longer thought about joining the Army. All he wanted was to get back home as soon as possible. One day he lay in wait for Pharnaces who was on one of his regular visits to the camp to receive orders.

"I'm coming back with you, *now,* Pharnaces," he informed him.

Pharnaces shook his head.

"Not possible, Rutilius. The Isis is no fit place for you at the moment. You would only be in the way and could get hurt. Some decking planks have sprung but, as soon as they're repaired, I'll send the boy for you."

Marcus watched him walk away. He did not trust him but there was nothing he could do about it. He had given up any attempt to see Caesar.

When he got back to the tent that night he found that Gaius Flaccus and the other men had been removed to the hospital and the men who had taken their places made it clear they were not happy sharing a tent with an outsider. He was, therefore, thankful to be kept busy. From time to time he saw Caesar in the distance working alongside his men. They all retired to their tents at night cold, wet and exhausted. Marcus got to the point where he could not remember doing anything other than carry wood from one place to another, hold planks in place as they were hammered to hulls and run messages. Was there such a place as Rome? And if so, would he ever see it again?

At last such ships as were salvageable were almost repaired and Marcus dared to hope that one day soon they would set sail away from this dreadful Island.

One morning Marcus woke to the sound of trumpets to find the men in the tent busily fastening on their weapons.

"What's happening?" he asked, apprehensively.

"There's going to be a battle – I should keep out of the way," one of the men replied, curtly.

When he found himself alone in the tent Marcus panicked. He was terrified. He did not want to witness more killing. He rushed from the tent. The sentry made no attempt to stop him as he ran out through the camp gate and into the woods. He ran until he was exhausted then took refuge in a hollow tree and settled down to wait. He could see very little through the trees but could hear the British chariots, the blast of innumerable trumpets and the shouted war-cries of the British.

Suddenly he heard shouted orders and the trumpets of the Legions. After that there were confused shouts and screams, he could not tell whether they were Romans or Britons dying, it all sounded the same – death was death. After a considerable time an eerie silence descended broken occasionally by what sounded like large animals crashing through the woods. Marcus remembered what Pharnaces had told him about the dreadful monsters that inhabited this island and burrowed down deeper into the leaves to await events. Once it was dark he tried to sleep but could not. What was happening? Had the Romans managed to rout the Britons or, Mars forbid, had the Romans been defeated? It was very quiet.

At last the light began to grow and he decided he would pluck up his courage and go back to the camp. There was no sound except the wind in the trees and the birds waking up. The battle was over, one way or the other.

Cautiously he left the tree and made his way through the wood. Still no sign of either Roman or Briton. When he eventually came out of the wood he looked towards the camp. There were no tents, no men, no warships on the beach. The sea was completely empty – the army had gone!

How dare Pharnaces go without him! All his possessions were on board The Isis of Geminus. By Pollux! when he caught up with the Captain he would make him smart!

Then, as he looked at the deserted camp, his anger drained away and he felt helpless and alone. Knowing how to survive on the streets of Rome was no preparation for the situation in which he now found himself.

Giving way to total panic he ran down to the beach and up and down the shore. It was not until his foot slipped on a pebble and he fell painfully onto his knees that he came to his senses.

As he sat getting his breath back he saw something bobbing in the sea. Getting to his feet he waded into the water to see what it was. It was one of the small boats. Here was a way to get home he thought excitedly. All he had to do was to get into the boat, point it in the direction of the continent and let the sea do the rest. He tried to remember odd scraps of conversations he had overhead on The Isis. Something about tides? He could not bring the conversation to mind. Probably didn't matter anyway.

He pulled the boat up onto the beach. He remembered the boy using oars. He searched the boat but there were no oars and no sail. Well, it would just take longer. He began to make plans. He could manage without food but must have drinking water. He had to find a container. He regretted leaving his cloak behind in the camp – he only had the tunic he stood up in, perhaps he could find something at the camp. Making his way back to the camp he managed to find a discarded water bottle but was unsuccessful in finding a cloak – everything had been taken. Once he had filled the water bottle from the stream running outside the camp he felt ready.

Sending up a prayer to Neptune he jumped into the boat and paddled with his hands until he was clear of the shore. After some time he glanced back over his shoulder to see how far he had progressed and was dismayed to find that he was drifting parallel to the shore. With some difficulty he managed to turn the boat towards the open sea and renewed his efforts. He had to get back to the continent before dark. He realized it was going to take longer than he thought. He was greatly encouraged to find when next he checked he was further out. He paused to take a drink from his water bottle. Not long now and he would be home!

The sea seemed to be taking him in the right direction at last. He would rest and then continue paddling. Lying down in the bottom of the boat he was soon asleep. He dreamt that he was in the baths in Rome then woke with a start to find the boat filling with water. Frantically he began to bail out using his bare hands but seemed to make little headway. The boat was moving in a most uncomfortable manner. The wind had freshened and the waves were much higher than before. Where was he? It was getting dark but, looking ahead, he could just make out trees against the sky. He must be home at last! He was drifting into a small bay and the boat was sinking. The boat gave a lurch and he was flung into the sea. With great difficulty he pulled himself up onto the rock on which the boat had foundered. He lay, too tired to move, and drifted in and out of sleep.

At dawn he woke feeling stronger. He was cold, his tunic was damp and his boots had gone. He got to his feet. By Hercules he was stiff! Every muscle ached. He had to find out on which part of the continent he had landed. He looked round and discovered that he was on a rocky promontory, one of two which enclosed the bay. He was bitterly disappointed when he realized that the trees he could see on the cliff top were the oaks of Britain and not the cypresses of Italy.

After some thought he decided that his first objective must be to find a way up from the beach. Once he had achieved that he would plan his next move. Some time later he found a path which appeared to lead up to the top of the cliff. After a steep and exhausting climb, made worse by his lack of footwear, he reached the cliff top and sank down on the turf to rest his feet which were bleeding. Then the sun came out and he began to feel warm for the first time in days. As he sat, half asleep, he heard the sound of horses' hooves on the turf and half turned round but it was too late. Something hard hit him on the head and everything went black.

When he surfaced he found he was wrapped in furs and lying on a bed.

He tried to get up and groaned.

"Awake, are you?" a voice said. "We thought you were a dead 'un!"

The man came closer. In the light of the fire in the middle of the hut Marcus was overjoyed to see a Roman soldier. He started up in spite of the fact that his head was about to fall off.

"Caesar is back – thank the gods!"

To his dismay the soldier shook his head.

"No, Caesar is not back – yet. He'll come never fear. He looks after his men."

There were murmurs of agreement from several shapes which moved and stretched and finally resolved themselves into more men.

"Where are we?"

Marcus asked.

"In the settlement of a Barbarian called Segotrix. Thinks he's a King. We were all captured in the last battle."

"What are they going to do with us?"

"No idea."

The soldier did not sound very worried.

He studied Marcus's clothes.

"From one of the ships are you?"

Remembering Livius's strictures Marcus nodded and the man seemed satisfied.

"You go back to sleep now, you need your strength."

Marcus fell into a fitful doze. From time to time he was conscious of voices and movement. Sometime during the day he was woken by someone binding his feet with strips of cloth and offering him food.

"Nothing like you are used to and only water I'm afraid but it'll keep your strength up."

The man stood over him until he had finished. The bread was stale and the water tasted bitter – British water was not a patch on Roman he decided.

Soon after he fell into a heavy sleep. He awoke feeling heavy-headed to find the hut in darkness only relieved by the fitful light from the fire which was very low. Gazing round, he saw that the hut was empty except for a man lying in the doorway. Quickly he rose and, taking a brand from the fire, hobbled over to find the man was dressed, not in the uniform of the Roman Army but the colourful clothes of the Celt and the Celt was dead.

Raising the firebrand above his head Marcus walked round the hut until he found the man-sized hole which had been punched in the wattle and daub wall at the point where the thatch was lower and the wall more vulnerable in consequence.

The men must have been planning the escape when he was brought in he thought, resentfully. Now he knew why the water had tasted so bitter – they had put something in it. Once they knew he was not in the Army they didn't care what happened to him. But, since it was still dark, they couldn't have gone very far. He would follow them and when he caught up with them he would demand that they take him with them.

He crawled through the opening. The night was cold but clear. No moon but plenty of light from the stars. Still on his hands and knees he looked about him ready to retreat into the hut at the first sign of a Celt. All was silent. Cautiously he rose to his feet and studied his surroundings. The round hut he had just left was on the edge of the settlement close to the perimeter fence consisting of a high earth bank topped by what looked like a fence of interlaced wood. It was too high to climb and, in any case, he knew his feet were in no condition to attempt it.

He could see no evidence of the earth bank having been climbed so the men must have found a gap in the fence. He began to creep along the bottom of the bank. He had not gone far when he heard a deep growl and a dog appeared. Marcus froze, so did the dog with his nose raised, sniffing the air. After some time he seemed satisfied and turning round trotted away. Marcus breathed a sigh of relief and continued his search until he came to a gap closed by a wooden gate. All he had to do was to go through the gate and he was free!

As he put his hand out to grasp the gate someone grabbed him by the collar of his tunic. He tried to wriggle free but was in a grip of iron, he could not move – the man was as strong as Hercules! Marcus was conscious of being dragged down the road between the huts until they halted in front of a hut much larger than the rest. Still grasping Marcus by the back of the tunic the man pushed him inside. After the darkness outside the blaze of light from torches set round the walls blinded him. He heard the murmur of many voices.

He was propelled to the rear of a circle of people sitting on wooden benches round the fire in the middle of the hut where his captor let him go. He stumbled and nearly fell. As he looked up he saw that he was standing in front of a man sitting on a large wooden chair. The walls of the hut were covered in bright coloured cloth on which shields hung at regular intervals. Marcus studied the man – this must be Segotrix. His fair hair came down to his shoulders and his long moustaches covered his mouth. The gold torc round his neck and the heavy gold bracelet encircling his powerful-looking wrist glinted as he sat forward to look at Marcus through narrowed eyes.

Segotrix rapped out a question addressed to Marcus's captor. Marcus could not understand what was said during the exchange except that his captor addressed the man as Segotrix thus confirming his suspicions that this was indeed the King of these Barbarians. Marcus was frightened but knew it was essential Segotrix did not realize this. Controlling his shaking legs with an effort and frowning, he drew himself up as he imagined Caesar would when confronted by an impertinent pleb. Segotrix looked at him intently then beckoned to three men who were standing in a group apart and said something ending with the name "Caesar!"Then, speaking in heavily accented Latin, Segotrix asked

"What is your name?"

Behind him Marcus heard the crowd gradually fall silent. In as firm as voice as he could manage he replied.

"Marcus Rutilius."

"You are a Roman soldier." Segotrix stated.

"No, I am not a soldier."

Segotrix gazed at him thoughtfully, then leaned forward and asked

"Are you related to Caesar?"

Marcus did not reply just gazed back at the Barbarian.

"His son, perhaps?" Segotrix persisted.

Marcus allowed himself an enigmatic smile. He was in a difficult position. If he acknowledged that he was some relation to Caesar, Segotrix might kill him, on the other hand Segotrix might be too afraid of Caesar to dispose of him so, until he knew what was in the Barbarian's mind, he thought it prudent to keep quiet.

Now one of the three men leaned towards Segotrix saying something in a low voice. Segotrix nodded and the man walked all round Marcus, peering at him intently. Marcus could do nothing but submit. After a final searching scrutiny the man returned to Segotrix and, bending down, whispered in his ear. Segotrix shrugged.

Marcus had no idea what was going on but decided to take a chance and spoke directly to Segotrix.

"When Caesar returns with his Legions you will pay for this indignity."

Segotrix smiled grimly and gestured to a man standing by his side. What now? Marcus wondered. The man went behind the wall hangings and reappeared seconds later carrying a small wooden chest which he placed on the table in front of the Chieftain. When Segotrix opened the box and produced a perfectly preserved head Marcus took an involuntary step backwards.

"This" said Segotrix, in the tones of one instructing a rather slow child, "is the head of a tribal chief who fought me and lost. One day I will fight and conquer Caesar and his head will join this one."

Marcus was badly rattled and hardly knowing what he was saying, shouted, "You Barbarian! Caesar will come with ten legions and you will be annihilated. Then you and the cowards who escaped and left me here will know what vengeance is!"

Too late he realized what he had said.

Segotrix suddenly became very still and, keeping his narrowed eyes on Marcus, gave an order. A man swiftly left the hut. Slowly and deliberately Segotrix put the head back into the chest, closed it and signalled to the man to replace it behind the hangings. Then he sat down and gazed steadily at Marcus. In the silence a child's clear voice could be heard asking a question. Still keeping his eyes on Marcus, Segotrix frowned heavily and the child was shushed. They waited, only the sound of breathing and the wood crackling on the fire breaking the silence. Marcus felt that his brain was about to explode. Segotrix was bound to take the men's escape out on him. Why had he been so foolish? A torch spluttered and Marcus jumped nervously. After what seemed a very long time the man returned, running, and shouted something to Segotrix. The Chieftain leaped to his feet shouting orders. For some moments there was confusion as the crowd rushed for the entrance. Segotrix grabbed one of the men as he ran past. Indicating Marcus he gave instructions. Turning to Marcus he said

"This man will take you to a hut. Once we have recaptured the Romans we will talk again. The man will stay with you to make sure you do not escape."

Marcus was led away to a much smaller hut than the one he had been held in previously. He tried talking to the Briton who stayed with him but the Barbarian had no Latin and only gave surly grunts while he sat and stared at Marcus by the light of the fire until Marcus could stand it no longer and laying down pretended to fall asleep but sleep was far away. He could not help remembering the dead Celt and had an uneasy feeling that, once Segotrix returned, he would kill him out of hand.

CHAPTER TEN

Marcus was in Rome watching Caesar's triumph. First came Segotrix in golden chains then, in a white chariot drawn by two white horses and wearing a purple toga, rode Caesar himself. A wreath of bay leaves on his head; his face painted red to represent Jupiter King of the gods. Marcus could hear above the shouts of the crowd the slave standing by Caesar's side whispering the customary warning "Remember, you are mortal!" Behind the chariot marched columns of soldiers holding sprays of laurel and chanting bawdy songs in praise of their Commander.

The cheers were deafening. The people lined the streets in their thousands. Caesar leaned towards Marcus and said something that was inaudible above the noise of the crowd. Marcus shook his head and Caesar leaned closer and began to shake his shoulder.

Marcus woke to find the Barbarian shaking him and making signs for him to get up. Pale daylight filtered into the hut.

Stiffly Marcus struggled to his sore feet. As he was led out of the hut he vowed that if he ever got back to Rome he would never leave.

"Where are we going?"

Marcus was afraid – was he going to be killed?

The Barbarian, grasping his arm firmly, did not respond.

The settlement was a hive of activity as people went about their daily occupations. Scouring fleeces, mending the thatch on the hut roofs and, everywhere, dogs and children. One small boy began marching by the side of his escort. For the first time in their acquaintance Marcus's custodian smiled as he gently waved the child away.

When they entered Segotrix's hut Marcus was dismayed to see that one of the three men present was Flavius, one side of whose face was badly bruised, the eye swollen shut and his arms securely bound to his sides by his belt. Marcus was dismayed. It had not occurred to him that Flavius might be one of the men who had attempted to escape.

Flavius saw him and, in spite of his bound arms, moved towards him his face full of anger. Marcus hastily retreated. He had to speak quickly before Flavius could say anything to give Segotrix the impression that he had aided the men in their escape. He moved towards Flavius as if greeting an old friend.

"Thank Jupiter you are safe! I knew it was impossible to escape in these forests and I told Segotrix what had happened so that he could find you and bring you back. There are monsters out there!"

Flavius snorted and looked at Marcus with disdain.

"It was our duty to escape, monsters or no monsters, but what would you know about that? You're only a civilian after all."

Segotrix looked from one to the other.

"What is a civilian doing with the Roman Army?" he enquired.

Flavius shrugged but said nothing. Segotrix looked at Marcus, questioningly.

Marcus knew he had to come up with something convincing. He didn't know what Segotrix had in mind for Flavius and the other prisoners but it was sure to be unpleasant and he had no intention of sharing it.

"Well?"

Segotrix sounded impatient.

Marcus had a flash of inspiration.

"Caesar wanted me to be with him on this campaign. In fact," he added, greatly daring, "Caesar has decided that I am to be the first Roman Governor of this island."

Flavius stared at Marcus in disbelief.

"Caesar has to conquer us first!"

The third man spoke.

"My brother, Cingetorix." Segotrix stated. "This brings me to another point. Cingetorix does not believe that you *are* Caesar's son."

"Neither do I," Flavius said, forcefully, "in spite of Decrius Marcellinus and Lucius making such a fuss about it. The other men don't believe it either. If he *is* Caesar's son why did Caesar sail away without him?"

Clearly Flavius did not intend Marcus to escape whatever fate Segotrix had in mind for him.

Marcus knew he had no answer but help came from an unexpected quarter.

"Because he had to retreat with no time to look for him. He probably thinks he's dead. Our warriors killed many Romans." Cingetorix sounded complacent. "Continue." He ordered.

Marcus was in no doubt that a great deal depended on what he was about to say. He knew from experience that the best lies should always contain more than a grain of truth. Taking a deep breath he began.

"My mother was a Vestal Virgin – do you know what it means if a Vestal breaks her vows?"

Flavius made as if to speak.

"Be quiet or I will have you removed."

Segotrix said, pleasantly. He looked enquiringly at his brother who shook his head.

"What is this Vestal and how can that prove you are who you say you are?" Segotrix frowned.

"The Vestals guard the eternal flame in the Temple of Vesta. If the sacred flame goes out Rome will fall."

"Then we shall make sure we extinguish it when we capture Rome."

Cingetorix promised, grimly.

"We also have sacred fires kept alive by the Druids."

Segotrix sounded mildly shocked that Romans could have similar beliefs.

"Continue, Roman."

"The virginity of the Vestals is paramount."

Marcus had never thought that all those years listening to Julia droning on about the Order might one day save his life!

"The Vestals live in a special house and once they are accepted they never see their families again."

"If they are so special how is it that you were born?" Segotrix asked, interestedly.

"After 30 years they are free to leave and get married if they wish. If they break the rule of chastity before this time they are buried alive and the man is flogged to death."

"And you call *us* Barbarians!" Cingetorix snorted.

Ignoring him Marcus continued

"After my mother left there was a scandal and four Vestals out of the six were accused of unchastity."

"What has this to do with your parentage?"

Segotrix sounded dangerously bored.

"I want you to understand the reasons for the tense feeling at this time. The people were convinced that something dreadful would happen to Rome if things were allowed to continue in so lax a manner. Soon after my mother left the order she met a Military Tribune who, apparently, promised her marriage. Caesar, for it was he, was already married at the time. I expect he intended divorcing his wife . . ."

"Or not!" muttered Flavius.

Marcus shot him a withering look and continued, "He then went back to his Legion promising to come back for her. Time went by with no sign of him then she discovered that she was pregnant. She had no doubt that the Tribune was the father. She was terrified because, due to the bad feeling against the Vestals at the time, she might be accused of unchastity *before* she left the order resulting in both their deaths. What she did not realize until long afterwards was that he had given her a false name. She would never admit that the man was Caesar since, until the day she died, she had an irrational loyalty to him in spite of his desertion and, by naming him, she could cause his death."

"Women are very strange." Segotrix mused.

"Caesar dare not acknowledge me even if he knew about me for the same reason. I was not told the truth until I attained adulthood at fifteen. More than one person has seen the resemblance, including Caesar himself, who still dare not acknowledge me openly."

Marcus finished, satisfied that he had stated a convincing case.

"So, what you are saying is that Caesar dare not acknowledge you openly for fear of being put to death?" Cingetorix asked.

Segotrix turned to Flavius.

"You're an ordinary citizen of Rome. Could all this be true?"

Marcus willed Flavius to believe him. Flavius stood, apparently deep in thought. Finally he spoke.

"I have seen Caesar's house, it is in the Subura – a very fashionable part of Rome. I have also seen the Vestals – all very young and beautiful women. There *was* a scandal involving the Vestals. My father told me about it."

It was at this point that Marcus knew his gamble had paid off – it was clear that Flavius had never been to Rome in his life – the Subura was one of the most unfashionable places it was possible to live in Rome. And as for the Vestals being young and beautiful – that was a joke. The youngest was six and the oldest over thirty. If he had not been so anxious he would have laughed aloud.

"So you now believe that this *is* Caesar's son?"

Segotrix leaned forward and studied Flavius intently.

"I'm not sure. Caesar is fair – Rutilius is dark but there *is* something about him that reminds me of Caesar," Flavius reluctantly admitted.

Marcus knew that if he could convince Flavius that would, in turn, convince Segotrix. If Segotrix thought he was Caesar's son he might think twice before he killed him. On the other hand it might have the opposite effect. He decided to take the gamble.

"I had a private interview with Caesar at Portus Itius during which he made it quite clear that he knew who I was."

"Why didn't you tell me this before?" Flavius asked.

Marcus, speaking in as anxious a tone as he could manage, which was not difficult, pleaded, "Flavius, Caesar made me swear never to tell anyone although I wanted to and you must swear by all the gods to keep this a secret – Caesar could yet be flogged to death!"

He ended, dramatically. He had no idea whether this was true or not but it did not matter – nobody was going to check and he knew that the Army worshipped Caesar. Flavius would not do anything to harm his Commander.

"I'm still not…" Segotrix cut across Flavius with an observation that made Marcus's blood run cold.

"I am sure Caesar has enough enemies who would be only too pleased to inform the Senate of this episode in his past."

Marcus slumped as he stood. He had gambled and lost – as usual!

Cingotrix stroked his moustache thoughtfully.

"If we get rid of Caesar there will only be another Roman eager to invade us. I would advise that we keep the Roman as a hostage against Caesar invading us in the future."

Marcus thanked the Gods that Cingetorix was more astute than Segotrix. But would Segotrix agree?

All three waited with their eyes on the Chieftain as he turned the suggestion over.

"Very well – I will send a message to Caesar that we have his son and if he invades his son will be handed over to the Druid for execution."

Knowing what Caesar's answer was likely to be, Marcus knew he had to escape before Caesar invaded.

Segotrix waved his hand to one of the two guards and Flavius was led away. No more was said. Marcus was returned to his hut by his guard.

Time dragged. Each day seemed longer than the one before. The weather turned colder. He discovered by dint of much labour that his jailor's name was Anamnus. He seemed a decent enough fellow for a Barbarian and he brought him some furs to keep out the cold, also some ointment to put on his feet which were soon completely healed. He and Anamnus sat for hours, one either side of the fire, neither able to communicate with the other. One day Anamnus had had enough and conveyed to Marcus that he would like him to teach him Latin so that they could converse. Marcus was quite happy to do so in his turn indicating that he would like to learn Celt. Anamnus was an able pupil and a good teacher so before long they were having conversations, albeit stilted, in a mixture of Latin and Celt.

Early one morning Marcus was conscious that Anamnus was trying to attract his attention. Why couldn't he let him sleep? Anamnus kicked him. Marcus took no notice, Anamnus kicked him again. With an irritated growl Marcus opened his eyes.

"Look what I have for you, Roman."

Anamnus sounded pleased with himself. He pulled someone from behind his back. It was young girl, naked to the waist as was customary for young unmarried Celt girls, her breasts painted with blue swirls, her skirt brightly coloured. Why was Anamnus so pleased to be showing him a Barbarian?

"She was captured by our warriors seven nights ago. She is of no value as she can't be sold. Segotrix was going to kill her but I persuaded him to let me have her. I thought she would cheer you up. You must miss having a woman."

Marcus looked at her. Anamnus expected him, Caesar's son, to sleep with this half-naked Barbarian!

"I don't think..."

Anamnus lost his temper and shouted, "She is a gift to you from me. I suppose it was too much to expect such a high-born *civilized* Roman to accept a gift from a *Barbarian!*"

Marcus realized that by refusing his 'gift' he had badly upset Anamnus who could make life difficult if he so chose. Perhaps it would not matter in the circumstances and it had been a long time...

Anamnus took the girl's arm saying, huffily, "I shall have to kill her then, she is no good to me."

"No, wait. I was just taken by surprise that's all. What did you say her name was?"

"I call her Simplicia. I don't know her real name."

"Have you asked her?"

"She can't hear or speak – that's why she can't be sold. She must have been perfect when she was born otherwise she would have been sacrificed. This often happens. The children get some sickness sent by the gods as a punishment that takes away their hearing. When we found her she was in a hut on her own and tied up so perhaps she was about to be sacrificed. Do you want her or not?"

"Yes, thank you, Anamnus, it was a kind thought," Marcus managed to say.

"Here she is then,"

Anamnus sounded mollified. Like all Barbarians his anger was quick but short lived. Marcus looked at the girl who was clearly very frightened. Marcus smiled, she tentatively smiled back. Marcus held out his hand.

"Come here."

Although she could not hear what he said she understood the gesture and slowly took his hand.

Some days later Marcus woke with a sore throat and a pounding headache. After making signs to Simplicia to stay with him Anamnus left to return some time later carefully carrying a beaker. He forced Marcus to drink the vile-tasting liquid. Marcus fell into a feverish doze only waking when Simplicia fed him more of the potion. After a few days he felt very weak but his fever had gone. To occupy his time he began trying to communicate with Simplicia. He mimed someone drinking. She hastened to bring him some water. He then went on to mime eating, going to sleep, feeling cold, feeling hot, everything he could think of. In a few days he was conversing with her although on a restricted level. When Anamnus also tried to communicate with her in the same way, she just stared blankly at him. Anamnus was furious.

"I'll beat her until she *does* understand!" He roared.

"No! You will not, Anamnus. She belongs to me. You gave her to me – remember?"

Anamnus snorted but said nothing only glared at Simplicia who moved closer to Marcus as if for protection.

When the weather became damp and foggy and Marcus huddled miserably over the fire shivering in his short tunic, Anamnus presented him with a woollen tunic, colourful breeches and a pair of leather shoes. Marcus took the clothes gratefully. Once he was dressed Anamnus inspected him and seemed pleased with the effect.

"You will need this."

He put a woollen hooded cloak round Marcus's shoulders fastening it with a round metal brooch.

"Thank you, Anamnus."

"It's Segotrix's orders – he doesn't want you dying from cold before he gets an answer from Caesar."

"Has there been no word?" Marcus asked, trying not to sound too anxious.

"No, and there won't be until the Spring."

So he was safe until the Spring. By then he would have formulated an escape plan. He noticed Simplicia watching them.

"Have you a cloak for Simplicia?" he asked.

"No, she's a Celt not a soft Roman. She is used to the cold." Anamnus replied, dismissively.

That evening, as they sat by the fire Anamnus remarked.

"It'll soon be Samain again."

"Samain?"

"To mark the change from Summer to Winter – the New Year. Don't Romans have such things?"

"We have many festivals. Our winter festival is the Saturnalia. There are great feasts, parties and gifts. Everyone looks forward to it."

"We have feasting and games. The Druid chants and there are recitations – and beer, plenty of beer."

"I'll enjoy that."

Anamnus looked doubtful.

"Segotrix may not let you take part. It is a time when the dead come from the Otherworld and move among us. They may not like a Roman being present. The gods could curse the crops and bring disease to the cattle and the people if we displease them."

"You'll go, of course."

Perhaps whilst they were all drunk, and he knew how much Anamnus enjoyed his beer, he and Simplicia could escape. He knew if he left her behind Anamnus would kill her and he now realized that he was quite fond of her.

"Segotrix has not given me any orders yet."

This could be the opportunity he was waiting for. He almost confided in Simplicia but decided against it – communicating such a complex idea by mime would be far from easy or secret and he was not sure how much Anamnus understood.

The first day of the Festival arrived. He had hoped that Segotrix would let Anamnus attend but Anamnus reported that he had been told he could not.

"I wish I could see the horse racing but Segotrix has ordered me to stay with you."

He grumbled.

Marcus had a sudden and unwelcome thought.

"You say that the dead walk the earth at this Festival?"

"Yes, they do."

"I don't want to meet my mother and Murdia. I didn't give them the proper burial rites. They'll never forgive me, especially Murdia."

"Is that all! Never fear Roman, this is a *Celtic* feast and you are *Roman*. I'll ask the Druid to make sure."

"No, don't do that, Anamnus. I'm sure you're right."

He did not want to bring himself to the attention of the Druid.

"Drink your beer and forget about it." Anamnus advised.

That evening, as they sat round the fire, a sudden glow lit up the hut doorway.

"They have lit the bonfire." Anamnus said excitedly. "Now we must extinguish the fire.The Druid will bring a brand from the sacred bonfire so that we can re-light the hearth fire."

Soon afterwards Anamnus went to the door and returned carefully carrying a burning stick of wood.

All next day as they sat in the hut they could hear the sounds of laughter and singing. Anamnus became morose only partly cheered by the frequent mugs of beer which were brought to him. At first he shared them with Marcus but, as the day wore on and the sounds of revelry became more frenzied, he drank alone.

CHAPTER ELEVEN

The next day was even worse until a Celt appeared in the doorway during the afternoon bringing them a large platter of food and plenty of beer for both of them. He said something to Anamnus which seemed to cheer him up considerably.

"Segotrix wants you to go to the feast tonight," he said as he divided the food into two.

"What about the dead?" Marcus asked fearfully.

"They went back to the Otherworld at dawn so you are perfectly safe."

"In that case I shall look forward to it." Marcus replied as he shared his food with Simplicia.

The rest of the day was taken up with preparations. Anamnus washed and braided his long hair. He offered to help Marcus braid his but Marcus insisted on Simplicia cutting his hair, which had grown to his shoulders. He also insisted on shaving. He might, from necessity, have to dress like a Celt but he was still a Roman and intended to look like one. Finally they were ready.

As they began to leave Simplicia began to walk with them to the hut entrance but Anamnus barred her way.

"NO!" he shouted.

Simplicia looked at Marcus.

"Can't she come too, Anamnus?" he asked.

"No, she is a slave. Besides," he shuffled his feet, tugged at his moustaches, looked all round the hut.

"Anamnus, look at me!" Marcus ordered. "Why can't Simplicia come?"

"You remember I said Segotrix had given her to me?" Anamnus stared over Marcus's head.

"Yes."

"Well, he doesn't exactly *know* he has. In fact" he said in a rush "he told me to kill her. There, now you know," he a said, defiantly. "I thought she would be company for you."

Marcus was touched. He realized that Anamnus had not only failed to carry out a direct order from his Chieftain but, by allowing a less than perfect person to live, had broken one of his culture's strongest taboos. It was a very long time since anyone had done anything for him without expecting something in return.

"Thank you, Anamnus. That was very kind. But surely Segotrix has seen her going about the settlement?"

"Probably but he would not take much notice of a woman carrying out her tasks and she just looks ordinary, nothing special."

Marcus had to agree that Simplicia was not the most beautiful woman in Britain.

"So you think that in an intimate situation like a feast where people are bound to speak to her she would be in danger?"

"I'm sure of it."

"Does she know this?"

"How can she? You're the only one she takes any notice of."

Marcus nodded and signalled to Simplicia that he wished her to stay in the hut then, ignoring her gesture of protest, left with Anamnus.

From the noise coming from the central hut the feast was in full swing. As he entered, a fight was in progress between two burly Celts urged on by Segotrix, resplendent in a magnificent gold torque and many arm rings. Sharing his elevated position at one end of the hut were four other men similarly attired in the torques of tribal leaders. Clearly this was a very important feast. Marcus wondered why he had been summoned. He knew the fate of a prisoner summoned to such a feast in Rome – death.

Segotrix saw him and beckoned him to come forward. Once Marcus reached him he indicated that he was to sit by him, Anamnus sitting on Marcus's other side.

"Welcome, Roman," he said, jovially. "Here," he held out a goblet. "Have some of our British beer."

"Do you have any Falernian wine?" Marcus asked, politely.

Segotrix roared with laughter.

"No, Roman, you will have to make do with this."

Thrusting the goblet into his hand he watched as Marcus tentatively tasted the brew. It was horrible.

Marcus remembered with nostalgia the feast they had had in Rome at the New Year. If Jupiter Optimus Maximus himself had told him then that he would be celebrating the New Year again within the year, in Britain, surrounded by Barbarians he would never have believed him!

"Good – better than your fancy wine, eh Roman?"

Marcus smiled thinly while resolving to get rid of it as soon as possible.

"I have a treat for you, Roman."

He roared something in Celt. The fight finished and an old man came forward carrying a small stringed instrument.

Segotrix waved his hand and the old man began to sing in a surprisingly youthful voice. Marcus could not follow all the words but gathered it was about Segotrix defeating the Romans in battle and capturing Caesar's son after single combat which went on for two days and nights. Marcus glanced at Segotrix who was beating time and nodding. He evidently believed every word. The old man finished amid enthusiastic applause.

"More beer!"

Segotrix waved to a woman who hurried to fill his goblet which he held out to Marcus who shook his head.

"Our beer not good enough for you, Roman?" Segotrix said, angrily.

Marcus took the goblet and forced some down. It did not taste quite so bad. Several hours later Marcus was wondering why he had thought it so revolting.

The Druid chanted a long and complicated song to much applause. It was not to Marcus's taste but he applauded with the rest.

Some women brought out baskets of apples. Anamnus leaned over to Marcus saying, "The apples are used for divination."

"How can apples foretell the future?" Marcus asked.

Anamnus explained.

"You take the apple, peel it – the peel must not break that is most important – then you throw the peel over your left shoulder and the shape it takes foretells your future."

Marcus was interested – perhaps he could find out exactly what it was the Sybil had hinted at. He watched as first one then another man or woman took an apple and, with fierce concentration, began to peel it. Not everyone managed to keep the skin intact but those that did threw the peel over their shoulder and studied the result amid heated debates over the shape the peel had taken.

Anamnus took an apple, peeled it and threw the peel over his shoulder. Studied the shape then put his foot on it but not before Marcus had noticed that the shape it took looked remarkably like an "M". Segotrix, who was well on the way to complete intoxication, laughed and slapped Anamnus on the back.

"You're destiny is tied up with the Roman, Anamnus, let's hope to your advantage!"

Anamnus did not look very pleased but said nothing.

"Now its my turn." Marcus stretched out his hand for an apple. Segotrix took his arm.

"I think not, Roman. These are our gods, not yours."

Marcus felt inclined to argue but at that moment a fierce fight broke out between two women and Segotrix dropped Marcus's arm and turned his attention to the better entertainment.

Eventually the party was over. Segotrix was snoring loudly and there were bodies scattered all over the floor. Marcus was disgusted to see many of them were women. Such a thing would not be allowed in Rome. These Barbarians had no sense of decency. Any Roman woman who became drunk in public was, quite rightly, put to death by her nearest male relative.

Unable to find Anamnus, Marcus began to make his way unsteadily to his hut. Halfway there he realized that he was, for the first time since being captured, on his own. Now might be a good time to escape but he needed a rest first. He looked for his hut which seemed to have suddenly disappeared, then finding it at last, he flung himself on his bed, pulled up his furs and passed out.

He woke next morning to a blinding headache and looked round for Simplicia to get him something to ease the pain. She was nowhere to be seen.

Anamnus was sprawled on the floor. Next to him was a large piece of wood. Marcus tried to make sense of it but there was a hive of bees in his head so he went back to sleep. He woke to find that the fire was out and it was freezing cold. Anamnus was groaning and trying to get up. Where was Simplicia? How dare she let the fire go out! He was very angry with her.

"Where is Simplicia?"

Anamnus did not answer but concentrated on getting to his feet. Marcus saw a large lump on his forehead and a suspicion began to form in his mind.

"What happened here last night? Did you come back and attack Simplicia?" he asked, furiously.

"She is only a slave. I could have her killed whenever I wanted and you couldn't do a thing about it. You are a captive, *Roman.*"

"Where is she?"

"I don't know. I expect she has run away."

Marcus turned away in disgust. He had thought that Anamnus was different and had benefited by contact with a civilized Roman but these Barbarians would never change. He turned his back on Anamnus and refused to speak to him even when, towards nightfall, Simplicia returned, dirty and exhausted. When Marcus questioned her as to where she had been she either did not understand or chose not to, it was difficult to determine which. After several unsuccessful attempts he gave up.

One day they woke to find thick frost everywhere. Then it began to snow. The road through the settlement soon became choked. Moving was impossible except for the most urgent tasks. Anamnus left Marcus and Simplicia together saying he had permission from

Segotrix to be with his family as it was obvious that even a Roman would not be foolish enough to try escaping in this weather.

To pass the time, Marcus tried to hold some sort of conversation with Simplicia other than on the subject of drink or food. It was impossible and he gave up in disgust and sat hunched up staring into the fire.

Simplicia touched his arm. Once she was sure she had his attention she took a piece of half-burnt wood from the fire, pushed aside the floor rushes and began to draw on the chalk floor. Intrigued, Marcus left the fire and studied her drawing. It was a goblet. She pointed to the goblet and then began to move her fingers then pointed once more to the drawing. Marcus had no idea what she was trying to convey. Then she drew another goblet only this time it was upside down. An empty goblet, that much was clear. She moved her fingers and again pointed at the drawing. Suddenly Marcus realized what she was doing – she was drawing in the air! All day long they practised "talking" in the air. Once they had mastered the everyday things Simplicia took him on to ideas. This was much more difficult. She began once again with the goblet then rapidly fluttered her fingers.

"Hot!" Marcus shouted.

They worked together until they could hold a conversation of sorts using only their hands. They practised all that day and the next becoming more and more proficient until they could hold quite long and complicated conversations. Towards evening Marcus tried to tell her about Rome. The buildings, the baths, the statues, the temples. He did not know how much she understood but it made him feel better just talking about it. She seemed to pay more attention when he began to describe the clothes and jewels that the women wore.

"Such beautiful material, Simplicia – silks from China, woven with gold thread, and the jewels! Necklaces of gold, pearls, emeralds, semi-precious stones. You would love it. Have you ever had a necklace or a finger ring?"

Simplicia shook her head.

"No jewellery at all – not even a bracelet?"

Again she shook her head.

"I'll take you back to Rome with me and buy you all the jewels you want. I'll become a Senator and we will have a grand villa on the Palatine and dozens of slaves. We'll give very grand dinner parties. Would you like that?"

Simplicia shook her head and signed that she wanted to go back to her tribe. Marcus thought he had misunderstood and asked her again but she signed "No!" and shook her head, vigorously.

"But you will be killed if you go back. When Segotrix found you you were tied up ready for sacrifice!"

Marcus could not understand how she could turn her back on the luxurious life he was offering her.

Simplicia became so agitated that he could not tell what she was signing.

"Slow down!" he ordered.

After some time he managed to get the gist of it. Apparently she was not a member of the tribe they found her with. She had been captured from a tribe much further North. She wanted to go back to be with her own people where she was known and accepted. Marcus tried once more.

"But surely you don't *like* living on this damp island? True, Rome is cold in the winter but in the Summer it is warm, warmer than the summers here. Come with me Simplicia – I'll even marry you, I promise!" He said, and almost meant it.

She shook her head, but Marcus was sure that, once they had escaped, she would change her mind. She just needed time to think about it, that was all.

A few days later a quick thaw set in with rain which turned the settlement road into a quagmire. The thaw was followed by more snow and it became much colder. Fresh food became scarce, the nights longer. The depressing weather was relieved by feasts at which there was always a plentiful supply of beer. Marcus was sometimes invited to these feasts and always made sure that he knew where

Anamnus was at all times. He did not want Anamnus, who always got extremely drunk, to repeat his attack on Simplicia.

Segotrix had swift changes of mood and would be quite jovial one minute only to turn aggressive the next. Marcus learnt that it was best to be as inconspicuous as possible on these occasions. One day Marcus woke to find an unknown Briton on guard who thrust him back into the hut and stood blocking the entrance making it impossible to see out.

When Anamnus arrived he was unable to meet Marcus's eye. Eventually he told him that the Druid had decided that the prisoners would be sacrificed to the tribal god to conserve the food until the men could go hunting again. Marcus felt very frightened at this news. Anamnus, realizing this, was quick to reassure him that Segotrix had insisted that Flavius and Marcus were not to be killed.

"The Druid was not very pleased but in the end he agreed that you and your friend would be spared."

"What will happen to the others?" Marcus asked.

"They are to be drowned."

Marcus was very relieved. He was confined to the hut but could hear the noise – shouting and trumpets which gradually faded into the distance.

The Winter was long and hard with frequent snow. People became thin and nearly everyone suffered from colds. Marcus thought the Winter would never end but, at long last, as the nights began to draw out and the weather became milder, the settlement came to life once more. The food improved as the men and dogs were able to go out and hunt. Marcus became restless and sent a message to Segotrix by Anamnus asking if he could see him. He waited impatiently for several days and finally Anamnus took him to Segotrix's hut where he found the Chieftain in a heated debate with Cingetorix which he broke off when he saw Marcus saying, "Anamnus tells me that you are unhappy with us, Roman."

Marcus tried to judge his mood.

"I just feel that I would like to do something to contribute to the life of the settlement. Work in the fields perhaps?"

If he could once get outside the settlement he was sure he would be able to escape.

"Very well," Segotrix agreed, much to Marcus's amazement. "Anamnus will tell you what to do."

He then turned back to resume his conversation making it clear that the audience was at an end.

Marcus was delighted. Now all he had to do was to perfect his escape plans.

"How soon can we begin work, Anamnus?" he asked as they walked back to their hut.

"Tomorrow."

"What will I be doing?"

"Are you a skilled thatcher?"

"Of course not."

"Can you repair a hut wall?"

"No".

Marcus was becoming despondent.

"There must be something I can do."

"Looks as if it is going to be clearing out ditches."

"Clearing out ditches! I thought perhaps some work in the fields?"

"Not outside the settlement, Roman. Too risky."

Marcus was bitterly disappointed but hoped that, in time, he could persuade Anamnus there was no risk of his escaping. He was not pleased at being given what he considered to be slave's work but he had asked for something to do.

At first he found the work very tiring but gradually got used to it and began to feel fitter than he had ever felt in his life. He slept well and his appetite improved. He would need to be fit if he was to carry out his escape plans.

As they worked he asked Anamnus many questions about the life of the settlement. He needed as much information as possible.

There were ditches everywhere and Marcus became acquainted with most of them. No sooner had one ditch been cleared than another needed attention. This gave him an opportunity to study the layout of the settlement, vital information when formulating an escape plan. The huts were some distance apart from each other and built either side of a wide grass road running from one side of the settlement to the other. There were pens for the sheep and cattle which supplied most of the settlement's needs – milk, meat and wool for clothing. He was particularly interested in the perimeter fence which ran round the entire settlement.

The settlement side of the fence was high but, now his feet were no longer raw lumps, he thought he would be able to climb the earth bank, however, the wooden fence on the top, in spite of only being made of regular posts interwoven with hazel rods, could prove difficult especially as he would have to escape at night. He had reluctantly decided that climbing the fence was the best plan when Anamnus took him outside the settlement to clear the deep ditch running round the foot of the fence on the other side and he realized that even if he did negotiate the fence he could injure himself badly by falling into the ditch.

It looked as if his only chance of escape was through one of the entrances so he turned his attention to the many comings and goings. Women regularly went down to the river to fetch water, men took their dogs out hunting, wagons went out to the fields. An escape during the day would be impossible. Next he studied the terrain. A grassy hill rose behind the settlement on top of which was a cluster of trees. If he could get up the hill without being seen he could hide in the trees.

"This is very different from Rome, Anamnus."

"I've never seen Rome and have no wish to."

Anamnus followed Marcus's gaze as he studied the trees, trying to calculate how far he would have to go before he got to their cover.

"Those trees are where the Druid carries out the Rites. It is a sacred place. Only the Druid goes there."

"This Druid seems to be very powerful," Marcus remarked.

"The Druid is very powerful. He has the gift of healing and can tell the future." Anamnus said, in awed tones.

As they resumed their labours Marcus turned over a plan. If he could only get to those trees Segotrix would not dare to send anyone in after him. The thought of the Druid did not bother him in the least. He was sure he could easily dispose of him if necessary.

As they walked back to the settlement Marcus's attention was caught by a man. It was not the man so much as the reaction of the people when they saw him that intrigued him. Mothers pulled their children out of his way, and everyone turned their back on him.

"Who is that?" Marcus enquired.

Anamnus spat on the ground. "Don't look at him. He is an outcast."

"Why?"

"He has been banned by the Druid."

"For what reason?"

"You do ask a lot of questions. I told you, the Druids have a great deal of power and you don't go against them. Now don't ask any more questions. I'm hungry – I want to eat, not talk."

Marcus became obsessed with turning over escape plans. After much thought he had decided what form it would take but not how to carry out his scheme. He had noticed that the chariots were brought inside the settlement perimeter at night. Where were the horses? He had a vague plan of stealing a horse. Where he would go and how he would survive he didn't yet know but knowing Celt must be an advantage.

Anamnus seemed to be related to everyone in the settlement one way or another. His favourite was the child who had marched by his side when Marcus first arrived. Marcus learnt that his name was

Cunobelin and was some close relation of Anamnus but how close Marcus could not work out.

Cunobelin often came and talked to Anamnus while they were working. Marcus was quite proficient in the language by now although he still made the odd slip much to Cunobelin's delight. Marcus discovered that Cunobelin's one ambition was to become a charioteer.

"Where do you come from?"

Conobelin asked as he sat watching them clear out yet another ditch.

"Rome – I am a Roman."

To Marcus's astonishment the child jumped up and ran away.

Marcus was puzzled.

"Why did he do that?"

Anamnus heaved a rock out of the ditch and onto the bank before he explained, "The mothers tell the children that, if they don't behave a Roman will catch them and eat them."

"But that's not true!" Marcus was indignant.

Anamnus shrugged. "I expect Roman mothers tell their children that the Barbarians will get them and eat them and that's not true either."

"Why do people make up these stories?"

Anamnus grunted. "I don't know but it has always been so."

It was several days before Cunobelin plucked up the courage to speak to him again. Remembering the child's passion Marcus asked, not looking at him but apparently concentrating on cutting himself a slice of meat,

"So you want to be a charioteer?"

The child struggled with the desire to talk about his passion and his horror that he was talking to a Roman and his passion won.

"Yes, I will be a charioteer one day."

"When?"

"Anamnus says I must get bigger before I can capture horses but I'm big enough now."

As casually as he could Marcus enquired, "Where are the horses? I never see them."

"They roam around in the forest and we capture them when we need them. Anamnus says…"

There was an angry growl from Anamnus who spoke angrily in Celt too rapid for Marcus to follow. Hanging his head the child walked away.

"Why are you angry with him? We were only chatting. I was not really listening I was just pleased that he was talking to me again. What was that he was saying about horses?"

"Nothing, he is obsessed with becoming a charioteer so that he can one day go out and kill Romans who ask too many questions."

Prudently Marcus did not pursue the matter.

"Well I am not really interested and no harm has been done."

As he went back to work, Marcus's head buzzed with plans. The days were getting longer and it was not as cold. He knew from questioning Anamnus that the fields around the settlement were bounded by ditches. These would need clearing. He had been with the Britons many months and had shown no sign of trying to escape. They were getting used to seeing him. Some of them even smiled and greeted him. If he could once get outside to the fields he could disable Anamnus in some way – perhaps with Simplicia's help – hide in the ditch then capture one of the horses and make for the trees on the top of the hill. Capturing a horse could not be very difficult. Cunobelin must have seen charioteers capturing their horses. He would pump the child when Anmanus was not about.

Unfortunately for Marcus's plans Anamnus did not leave the child alone with him. It was clear that he had been reporting back their conversations and had now had orders not to let Cunobelin part with any more useful information. Marcus was about to resign himself to a change of plan when, a few days later, a surly looking Celt came to the hut. He refused to answer Marcus's questions regarding the whereabouts of Anamnus.

When Marcus asked Cunobelin he told him readily enough

"He is talking to Segotrix and…"

The Briton took the boy by the arm

"Get out. Anamnus allows you too much freedom."

The child looked mutinous.

"When I am a charioteer you'll not dare speak to me like that!"

"You! A charioteer!" the man scoffed.

"One day I'll show you!"

The boy tearfully stumped out of the hut to the loud laughter of the Briton.

A short time after Anamnus returned. He refused to tell Marcus what Segotrix had wanted. Marcus knew he had to escape soon or it would be too late. Caesar's invasion fleet could be arriving any day now. He brought up the matter of working in the fields.

"After all" Marcus remarked "you will be with me all the time and I am sure that an extra pair of hands would be very useful."

"It is not up to me it is…" he stopped "Listen! What is all that noise – are we being attacked?"

The noise was coming from outside the settlement. People began to leave their various occupations and converge on the entrance. Marcus and Anamnus made their way to the back of the crowd. Perhaps this would be a good time to escape. Anamnus must have had the same thought as he firmly grasped Marcus's arm. The crowd parted and then fell silent as a man quickly strode through them carrying Cunobelin in his arms. The child was very still and white. There was blood dripping from a large gash on his forehead.

Anamnus pushed his way through the crowd, dragging Marcus with him.

"What happened?"

"He was trying to capture a horse and it kicked him in the head. Fetch the Druid!"

Several men ran out through the entrance.

Anamnus clutched Marcus's arm painfully. The crowd followed the man and Cunobelin to a hut where they vanished inside, the people crowding in the doorway.

Marcus tried to pull his arm away.

"Go to him, Anamnus" he urged.

Perhaps he could take advantage of the tragedy and escape.
"Come, Roman."

Anamnus pulled him roughly away from the crowd and marched him back to the hut where Simplicia, who was feeding the fire looked up in surprise. She looked questioningly at Marcus who shook his head and indicated that she was to continue with her work.

Anamnus sat down, got up, walked round the hut and peered out through the doorway.

"Where is the Druid?" he fumed.

"I'm sure he will be here soon. Why don't you go and see what's going on?" Marcus suggested.

If only he could get rid of Anamnus he and Simplicia might be able to slip away while everyone was occupied.

"Because I don't trust you, Roman." Anamnus replied.

"You could tie me up," Marcus suggested, helpfully.

"And have Simplicia release you? Oh no, I'm staying here."

He sat down on one of the benches by the fire and folded his arms.

Time wore on. Simplicia cooked their meal. Marcus ate ravenously. Anamnus left most of his. Once it was dark Anamnus left saying, "I must find out if Cunobelin lives."

When he came back he told them that the Druid had arrived but Segotrix had refused to let Anamnus see the boy.

Marcus and Simplicia went to bed but, instead of leaving them on their own to go to his own hut as he had always done since Simplicia came, Anamnus sat by the fire and he was still there when Marcus woke the next morning.

CHAPTER TWELVE

Anamnus sat without speaking. Everything was very quiet. The usual morning noises were absent. It was as if the entire settlement was holding its breath. Marcus went to the door of the hut but the only sign of life was a small child who came running out of one of the huts. A woman came after it, picked it up, put her finger to her lips to indicate silence and took it back into the hut.

Marcus could not stand Anamnus's silent misery any longer.

"Go and see what is happening, Anamnus. I give you my word as a Roman that I will not try to escape."

Anamnus looked doubtful then suddenly, making up his mind, ran from the hut.

He did not return until evening.

"Did you see him? How is he?" Marcus enquired.

"Segotrix still wouldn't let me into the hut. One of the women told me that the Druid is going to open his head."

"What do you mean, he is going to open his head?" Marcus was horrified.

"The Druid will make a hole in his head to help heal him."

Anamnus was matter of fact as if it was the most usual thing in the world to make holes in people's heads!

"He'll kill him! You must stop him!"

"No, no, it has been done many times before. Don't Roman physicians do this?"

"I have never heard of one making a hole in anyone's head!"

Seeing Anamnus's anxious face he added, "But that does not mean it would not work."

"The woman promised to tell me as soon as the operation was over. There's nothing we can do but wait."

Simplicia looked enquiringly at Marcus who made signs to indicate opening his head. She nodded and calmly returned to her cooking. These Barbarians seemed to put great faith in their Druid.

Marcus made a mental note to inform Caesar that a way to conquer these people might be through their Druids. Destroy the Druids and their power and the people would be without guidance.

Night came and there was still no word. Simplicia brought food which Marcus managed to persuade Anamnus to try and eat. There was still no word when they went to bed. Anamnus once again staying by the fire.

During the night Marcus dreamt of having his head cut open by a grinning Druid. He was woken early in the morning by Anamnus talking in low tones to someone at the door.

Anamnus finished his conversation and went back to the fire. Marcus got up and asked for news.

"The operation is over. Cunobelin has not spoken. There has been a meeting of the people. The Druid told them that he could do nothing more. Now it is up to the gods."

Anamnus fell silent but Marcus felt there was more – there was.

"Segotrix is distraught. Cunobelin is his only son. He must survive. The Druid says there is only one thing to do. The gods will have to be appeased."

Marcus had a nasty feeling in his stomach.

"Yes?" he was finding it difficult to breathe.

"There will have to be a sacrifice. It must be someone special."

Marcus felt faint.

"Segotrix wanted it to be you – Caesar's son – who better?"

Marcus gasped and went white.

"But the Druid said it must be a warrior and you are not a warrior."

Marcus breathed again, this Druid seemed quite sensible.

"Who?"

Although he already knew, he needed to hear it to be sure it was not himself.

"I'm sorry, Roman. I know you would have preferred to go to the gods to plead for Cunobelin."

Marcus tried to look noble. Not easy when he was overjoyed but he composed his features into what he considered to be a suitable expression and looked as disappointed as he was able.

"Of course but, as you say, I'm not a warrior and the gods would not accept *me* – I am not good enough."

Better leave it at that and not overdo it.

"So, it is to be Flavius then?"

Anamnus nodded.

"When?"

"As soon as the Druid has made all the arrangements. There is the pit to prepare, the arrows to make."

"Arrows? Pit?"

"The sacrifice is tied to a stake which has been placed in a special pit. Then our noblest warriors will shoot him with arrows made from the sacred tree."

"Why a pit?"

"Closer to the Underworld."

Marcus shuddered – Jupiter! what an escape! His inner voice accused him. You could have been far away from these Barbarians who sacrifice people if you had taken the opportunity when it was offered. A thought struck him

"Why must it be a human and not an animal? Wouldn't the gods be just as happy?"

"It has to be a human life for a human life – that is the law."

Marcus felt disgust. Unfortunately he let it show on his face. Anamnus suddenly became angry.

"I know it is not the *civilized* way a *Roman* would appease the gods but it is *our* way."

"I'm sorry, Anamnus. I did not mean to imply…It was such a shock, that's all."

"You'll be able to make up your own mind about it as the sacrifice needs to be made in public and you will have to be present." Anamnas said, sulkily.

Better to be spectator than participant!

Marcus had been living with these people for many months and he thought he knew them. But he did not. They were Barbarians and would never change. He must escape as soon as possible because, he suddenly realized, once Flavius had gone he was the only Roman left! They might decide they needed another Roman to take a message to the gods!

The harsh note of a trumpet interrupted his thoughts. He started back as Anamnus suddenly produced a length of rope from somewhere.

Simplicia ran and tried to snatch the rope away. Anamnus pushed her aside but she grabbed his arm. Marcus tapped her hand to attract her attention. She looked at him and he shook his head and smiled to indicate that he did not mind. In fact he was quite happy to have his captive status stated so obviously. He did not want to look as if he was taking part in the sacrifice. It was important that Flavius should not get the wrong impression. After all who knew what the dead could do? Flavius might appear to Caesar in a dream and name Marcus as conspiring at his death to save his own skin.

Anamnus began to tie his hands in front of him saying, "I'm sorry Roman but I must tie your hands. Segotrix insists, he is afraid that you will escape while everyone is watching the sacrifice. I told him that you had given me your word but he did not think that was good enough. Don't worry, I won't pull it very tight."

Anamnus finished tying the rope.

"Are you ready?"

Marcus nodded and was led outside. Simplicia trailing along behind them. Anamnus led them out of the hut to join the stream of people who were making their way out of the entrance and up the hill. Just before they got to the trees the people parted into two silent lines. Flavius, escorted by two warriors with drawn swords, walked between the lines. As he passed him, Marcus took a step back, he didn't want to meet Flavius's eye but Flavius stared straight ahead. They got to the pit and one of the Celts climbed down followed by Flavius, the other Celt bringing up the rear. There was a pause, the two Celts climbed out of the pit, removed the ladder and stepped back to join a line of men each with a bow and one arrow.

The Druid, an imposing figure in his long white robe, the golden disc on his breast flashing in the sun, his long beard and short hair in sharp contrast to the long-haired and moustached Britons, began an incantation in a strong, resonant voice. Then he lifted his arm and everyone responded with a shout. When he lowered his arm silence fell. Marcus felt a tingle of fear. Once more the Druid raised his arm. Marcus jumped as there was a loud blast on the trumpet and shut his eyes. There was a "whoosh" of arrows followed by a collective sigh from the crowd. Marcus opened his eyes to see the crowd quietly dispersing and the Druid disappearing into the trees. It was all over.

"It was a good death."

Anamnus sounded pleased. They made their way back down the hill to their hut where Anamnus untied his hands. Marcus wanted to do some work. Even clearing the ditch would be better than sitting, brooding. Anamnus shook his head.

"Not until tomorrow. The people are not all convinced that Flavius was the right choice. There could be trouble. Wait a few days. We should know by then whether the gods have accepted Flavius in the place of Cunobelin."

"And if they don't?"

"Better not think about that, Roman."

So, he was not safe yet.

The next few days seemed very long, but when Anamnus came bounding in one afternoon, grinning all over his face, Marcus knew he could breathe again.

"He has spoken!"

Anamnus was clearly overjoyed.

"Good! Now can we go outside?"

"Yes, tomorrow."

Marcus had thought that once he was working outside again he would feel less despondent. But the warmer weather reminded him of Rome and he woke one morning to no appetite and a feeling of depression. Nothing Anamnus could say or do to cheer him had any effect. He felt completely alone. He could be here for years. He could see no way out. He refused to eat.

"Do eat something, Roman."

"Why should I?" Marcus asked.

"I don't want you to die."

"What is it to you whether I die or not? To you I am just 'the Roman'".

"Because, if you die so do I." Anamnus said, hotly.

Now he had Marcus's attention.

"Why?"

"Segotrix told me when you first came that, if you escaped he would kill me, cut my body into pieces and feed it to his dogs."

"Why you?"

"Segotrix doesn't like me."

"Obviously, but aren't you some kind of relation?"

"My sister was Segotrix's wife."

"Was?"

"She died when Cunobelin was born. For some reason Segotrix is convinced that I am plotting to kill Cunobelin. I would never do that, I am fond of him, he reminds me of my sister. All this happened just as you arrived. When Segotrix consulted the Druid he decided that I could prove my loyalty by becoming jailor to an enemy of the Tribe – a Roman. If I allow you to escape I'm to be killed.

"What will happen to you when Caesar comes for me?"

Anamnus shrugged.

"When Caesar comes for you the Druid will order Segotrix to allow me full membership of the Tribe again as I would have finished my punishment."

Marcus knew that the only way Caesar would come for him would be with several Legions. As soon as Segotrix got word of the invasion he would kill him. Therefore, the only way Anamnus could lose would be if he escaped. If he stayed he would be killed, if he escaped Anamnus would be killed. He asked himself the question – would he care if Anamnus died? Yes, he would, but as things stood they couldn't both live. He sighed and threw down the bone he was chewing.

Seeing his despondent face, Anamnus tried to think of something to cheer him up. Then he had it.

"Tell me about Rome."

Hearing the word "Rome" Marcus looked up.

"Rome?"

"Yes, Rome – tell me about it. Is it a good place to live?"

"The best place in the world."

Marcus spent the rest of the evening telling Anamnus about the buildings, the temples, the streets, the baths, the shops, the people, the city life. He did not finish speaking until late into the night. He fell silent at last and then said

"I shall never see Rome again!"

Anamnus could see that he was ready to sink back into despair and hastened to reassure him

"Caesar must have had the message from Segotrix by now and, when the weather is right, he will come himself and negotiate with Segotrix. Then there will be no invasion and you can go home at last and I can go back to my normal life. Caesar is bound to do something soon. You are his son after all."

Marcus gave a thin smile. Yes, but am I? He had no real grounds for thinking he was Caesar's son. All the proof he had was a superficial resemblance between them. On the other hand, Caesar had taken notice of him and he had ordered Pharnaces to take him to Britain. He would not do that for just anybody. If Caesar did invade Segotrix would kill him so he must escape. If he could make his way to the coast he could wait for Caesar to arrive. But if he escaped Segotrix would kill Anamnus and Simplicia! Jupiter! What a mess! Then he had a bright idea – they could escape with him! It would be useful to have Anamnus to do the guiding and hunting and Simplicia to do the cooking. That way they could easily survive for months! The more he thought about it the more sense it made.

He was sure that, when the idea was put to them, they would be delighted at the prospect of living in Rome. He would make Anamnus his Chief Household slave and, when he got married, Simplicia would be his wife's personal slave. He was sure that once Simplicia saw the shops in Rome she would thank the Bona Dea for sending her such good fortune. He knew that all women liked to shop – look at Annia! But he needed something to give him access to Caesar. Something that Caesar would be so pleased to have that he would not only welcome Marcus but Simplicia and Anamnus as well even though they were Celts. Some information which only he could provide. Then he had it. He would take Caesar details of the British defences and also offer his services as an interpreter in any negotiations.

Yes, it was a good idea, best get started straight away.

Anamnus was delighted to see the Roman suddenly looking more cheerful. Getting him to talk about Rome had been a good idea. He would quite miss him when Caesar came for him.

Marcus spent the rest of the night mentally making a list of all the information Caesar was likely to require. From tomorrow he would begin taking a more careful note of everything that he saw and heard.

As he drifted off to sleep he remembered the words of the Sybil. If it was a true prediction then he would get home otherwise how could he become a great man of Rome? It was just a question of time. Sighing contentedly he rested his head on Simplicia's breast and went to sleep.

CHAPTER THIRTEEN

Having come to a decision regarding his future, Marcus quickly regained his usual confidence and resolved to put into immediate effect his self-imposed role as Caesar's spy.

They were busily clearing out the deep ditch by one of the entrances and Marcus was, as usual, taking note of all the comings and goings. He noticed that Segotrix seemed to be having a continuous stream of visitors. Turning to Anamnus he casually asked, "Why is Segotrix so popular suddenly?"

"I don't know. It's none of our business."

Marcus shrugged and turned back to his work as if satisfied but he was sure that something was going on. As Caesar's spy it was up to him to find out what it was but he could not think how. Anamnus seemed to be more attentive than ever and never left him alone for a second.

As the days passed he continued to think up ways of solving the mystery only to reject them.

One evening as they ate their meat Anamnus told him that Beltane, the feast to mark the first day of Summer, had arrived.

"Segotrix has given you permission to take part in the festivities." Anamnus informed him then went on.

"Tell Simplicia that I have decided that she can come but she must keep with us."

When Marcus told Simplicia about the plan she promised to obey Anamnus's orders. She told Marcus that she always enjoyed the celebration of the sun's return and went out on the evening before the feast to gather green branches with which she decorated the inside of the hut. A large bonfire was lit on the top of the hill. Two more fires were lit either side of the settlement entrance between which the cattle were driven. Anamnus explained that it would protect them from disease. Once again all the hearth fires were extinguished then re-lit from the sacred bonfire on the hill.

Everyone was out to enjoy themselves. They danced round the bonfire until they were exhausted. There was food and drink in abundance. The Druid gave yet more recitations. Segotrix saw Marcus where he sat next to Anamnus and called him over.

As he rose to his feet, Simplicia looked up in alarm. He shook his head.

Marcus hoped that Simplicia understood. He dare not use signing – if Segotrix discovered who she was he would probably kill her there and then and also make it an excuse to kill Anamnus for not carrying out his orders. He went over to where Segotrix sat, surrounded by men, who, from their dress and demeanour were important tribal leaders.

"Do they have such a spectacle in Rome?"

Segotrix asked.

"No." Marcus said, with perfect truth.

"When we conquer Rome we will teach you Romans how to live!"

Segotrix arrogantly replied and waved his hand in dismissal.

The men round Segotrix laughed. Segotrix sat back, satisfied that he had impressed his guests.

Marcus boiled with anger. One day he would come back accompanied by Caesar and his Legions – then Segotrix would regret his treatment of a Roman! He looked round at the crowd. Anamnus was deep in conversation with an elderly woman who seemed to be anxious about something. Seeing Marcus watching them Ananmus brought her over.

"This is my mother. She is worried that you will kill me."

"Greetings," Marcus said formally.

"Please don't kill my son, Roman" she begged. "He is all I have."

"I will not kill your son, Lady. I like him – he is my friend."

"Go back to your friends, Mother. I have to stay with the Roman."

Anamnus gently pushed her away. As they watched her go back to a group of women who were sitting gossiping Anamnas said.

"Thank you for reassuring her. She is old, she gets frightened. Come on – I want a drink. Where is Simplicia?"

"Over there, where we left her. We had better get back to her before somebody speaks to her."

As the evening wore on the beer began to flow more freely and couples began to disappear into the twilight. Marcus looked round for Simplicia. She had been sitting between himself and Anamnus. Now Anamnus was in a drunken sleep and Simplicia was nowhere to be seen. Marcus felt uneasy. Had she been discovered? Then he saw her briefly silhouetted against the flames of the dying bonfire, she was making her way up the hill. She looked back from time to time, then she was over the hill and out of sight. She had escaped. Marcus looked round at the drunken revellers to see if anyone else had noticed her departure but they were all oblivious to anything but their own concerns. He felt a mixture of sadness and relief, relief being uppermost. He would not now have to engineer her escape as well as his own. He was glad he had not taken her into his confidence. She would never have fitted in back in Rome. Caesar would not approve of his marrying a Barbarian and an imperfect one at that. He must keep Anamnus from finding out that she had escaped. He knew what Anamnus's first reaction would be – absolute fury and a determination to hunt her down and kill her.

For two days Anamnus accepted Marcus's various explanations for Simplicia's continuing absence then, on the third morning

"Where's Simplicia?"

"About somewhere, I expect."

Marcus casually replied but this time Anamnus was not satisfied.

"No, I've looked. The last time I saw her was at the feast. She escaped at the feast, didn't she? Did you see her go?"

"I was too busy trying to get you back down the hill."

"I'll get some men together. We'll take the dogs. When we catch her I'll kill her. Nobody makes a fool of me!"

Anamnus said, angrily.

"Is that a good idea, Anamnus? Remember that you have already killed her – at least that's what Segotrix believes. Let her go. I'm sure you don't want the Druid to become involved, do you? And he will if Segotrix finds out you've disobeyed him – again!"

At the mention of the Druid Anamnus began to calm down.

"I suppose you're right. Anyway she'll probably be captured by somebody before she gets home."

Marcus hoped she would not but only nodded and continued feeding the fire.

"If you will lend me your knife, Anamnus, I'll cut up the vegetables for the stew."

Anamnus took his knife from his belt and began to hand it to Marcus, then snatched it back again.

"No, Roman. How do I know this is not a plot? The girl escapes, hides in the woods, you kill me, wait until dark then you join her."

Anamnus would not listen to Marcus's protestations of innocence and attacked the vegetables as if they were Romans.

The next morning Anamnus announced that they would go and clear the field ditches.

Marcus was overjoyed. An opportunity to escape must surely come his way now but he knew that outside the settlement he would probably be even more closely watched so in order to make Anamnus think he had given up any idea of escape he made no attempt to do anything other than work, eat and sleep.

One of the fields in which they worked was on a slope above a flat stretch of ground. Three sides were bounded by dense woods, the fourth looked down the slope to a patch of flat ground on the banks of a wide river. The charioteers practised their manoeuvres on this piece of ground all day long. From time to time they drove their chariots into the shallow river and splashed about cooling their horses and themselves. If he could steal a chariot and ford the river he could get to the sea. Standing up and wiping his sweaty face on his sleeve, he pointed to the men in the river.

"They look nice and cool, Anamnus. Why don't we go down and join them?"

If Anamnus could be put into a position where it appeared that he was aiding Marcus to escape he would have no alternative but to escape with him or face the consequences.

"They like to keep themselves to themselves. Besides I don't intend getting run down by a chariot."

Marcus sighed. It was going to be more difficult than he had thought. He turned his attention to the dense woods bordering the field. Once in there he was sure he could disappear. What he needed was a diversion. How to achieve this occupied his mind for several hours. Whatever he was going to do it would have to be soon as in a few days time the ditches would be cleared.

Then, just after the midday rest a man entered the field, looked round and seeing Anamnus came over.

Anamnus straightened as the man approached the ditch and climbed out to speak to him.

Marcus realised that this was the chance he had been waiting for. He would have to leave Anamnus behind but he might be able to come back for him before Segotrix killed him. As these thoughts raced through his head he crouched down ready to run along the ditch as fast as he was able in the direction of the wood. The dangerous time would be when he had to leave the safety of the ditch and enter the woods. He prayed to all the gods to keep Anamnus occupied until he was safely hidden among the trees.

The man began to speak to Anamnus before he got to him.

"Anamnus" the man panted, he had obviously been hurrying "Segotrix wants you."

"Segotrix wants *me?*"

"Not just you, he wants the Roman as well. Where *is* the Roman?"

Marcus was several feet down the ditch when he heard this exchange. Grabbing up a rock he straightened up and threw it out of the ditch.

Anamnus turned to Marcus.

"Roman, we must go. Segotrix wants us."

Marcus idly scratched a gnat bite.

"Why?" he asked.

"No idea," the messenger replied, "but if I were you I would hurry. He's not in a very good mood!"

Grabbing Marcus's arm Anamnus began hauling him along the forest track to the settlement.

"Perhaps something has happened to Cunobelin!"

Anamnus was worried.

When they arrived, hot and panting, they found Segotrix fully armed, complete with ornate bronze helmet, pacing up and down outside his hut impatiently running his sword in and out of its scabbard. As they came hurrying towards him he gestured to them to hurry then turned and entered the hut. They followed, Anamnus pushing Marcus before him. Once inside Segotrix ordered Anamnus to stand by the door.

As Anamnus moved to the door Segotrix turned to Marcus.

"Roman, I have had word that Caesar is preparing to invade and as he has not replied to my message I see no reason to keep you alive. I will, however, kill you at the proper time. I want your father, if he is your father, to see *you* killed before I defeat and kill *him* in battle!"

Marcus was incapable of speech. He had never felt so frightened.

"Perhaps your information is incorrect. Your message has not arrived – there have been some very bad storms. Perhaps . . ."

Segotrix cut short his frantic babbling.

"See how brave your Roman is, Anamnus! This is the pathetic creature you pleaded with me not to keep bound as I intended."

He turned back to Marcus.

"Perhaps you are not Caesar's son after all in which case I see no reason why I should not kill you straight away!"

He drew his sword.

Marcus fell to his knees and, grovelling in the dirty rushes at Segotrix's feet, pleaded, "Don't kill me!"

He heard Anamnus snort of contempt but he did not care.

"If all Romans are like you we'll soon drive them back into the sea!"

Segotrix sneered.

To Marcus's intense relief he thrust his sword violently back into its scabbard.

"Take him to the fort, Anamnus. Make sure he stays there. I want him under my hand when Caesar arrives. He will die in front of Caesar, he may not be his son but he is a Roman, although a poor one."

He contemptuously prodded Marcus with his foot.

"Get up. Tie his hands, and keep them tied."

Anamnus pulled him to his feet.

"Coward!" he hissed.

As Anamnus pulled the rope tight until it cut into his wrists, Marcus knew, from the expression on the Barbarian's face that the friendship which had built up between them over all those months had dissipated.

At first he was deeply ashamed of his descent into abject terror. But then, as Anamnus hauled him along none too gently, he began to see that it was not such a dreadful thing. By the time they had left the settlement and climbed up to the fort he had begun to believe that it had all been part of his plan to deceive the Barbarians into thinking he was completely cowed. He congratulated himself on his acting. He was so good he had almost deceived himself!

He had been so busy communing with himself that he was inside the fort without really knowing how he got there. He was not given any food. The Briton did not speak to him or answer when he tried to start a conversation. After tying the end of the rope to a post outside one of the huts, Anamnus went and stood in the entrance to the fort. Night fell and Marcus could see him silhouetted against the light summer sky. He called out and asked for water: to be untied so that he could sleep in one of the huts: for an explanation: for some sort of answer, but Anamnus stood as if he had taken root, he neither answered nor moved. Marcus doubted if he even breathed.

Finally, just as the sun was coming up, Anamnus moved at last. Marcus was instantly alert and pricked up his ears. All he could hear was the sound of bees. Why would Anamnus be so interested in the sound of bees? The sound got louder, changed to a murmur, changed again to voices coming nearer. Anamnus disappeared through the gap then reappeared helping his mother up the last few feet of the slope. She was followed by dozens of people who flowed through the entrance. The women and children went into the huts and the men stood with drawn swords along the ramparts. Above the chatter of the people Marcus could hear the bellowing of cattle and the bleating of sheep. He saw a man he knew and called to him.

"What is happening?"

The man did not reply. Marcus tried several times to attract somebody's attention but it was as if he did not exist. Then he remembered the man in the settlement who had been totally ignored because he was a criminal and a coward. How dare they treat him like this! He pulled at his bonds but they were too tight.

Suddenly several men passed him heaving a large tree trunk which they placed across the entrance and after them came more men with more tree trunks until the entrance was blocked. Marcus tried to stand up, he knew what had happened – Caesar had arrived! There was an eerie quiet, even the birds were silent. Then he heard it – the sound of a marching army. He could not get up but he could imagine the sun shining on the helmets and lances of the Legions. How many Legions had Caesar brought? If only he could see! Suddenly the Britons shouted as one.

"Come, Romans! Come and fight!"

There was no reply. The Britons began hurling stones as well as taunts. After some time stones and arrows began to come over the ramparts. Marcus made himself as small as he could and covered his head with his arms. He was in an impossible position – he could be killed by a missile before the Romans captured the fort and if the Britons won Segotrix would carry out his resolve to kill him.

As if to confirm his fears, an arrow missed his head by inches and embedded itself in the wall of the hut. This gave him an idea. Gradually crawling towards the arrow he pulled it out of the wall and used the arrow head to saw at the ropes round his wrists. This took some time as he had to take cover every few seconds as more and more missiles came over the ramparts. He was sure he would soon be hit. At last the rope parted and he was free. As he debated where to go there was confused shouting from behind him. Creeping round the side of the hut he saw a sight which made him stand with his mouth open quite forgetting that he was in the midst of a battle. Pouring over the ramparts were Roman soldiers, hundreds of them. While the Britons had been kept occupied at the front of the fort the Romans had built a ramp at the back. The Roman Army was truly invincible! At last he could escape! He began to run towards the nearest Roman soldier but was pulled back.

"You are coming with me, Roman. Caesar can still be defeated."

Segotrix grasped him firmly. Marcus shouted but nobody could hear him above the noise of the battle. He struggled hard but Segotrix was too strong. Women and children began to run out of the huts and Segotrix and Marcus were carried along in the rush to leave the fort. Weaving their way in and out of the bodies of the dead and dying Britons the survivors poured out of a gap in the ramparts and fled down the hill to the woods. As dusk came the sky was lit by the glow of the burning fort.

As he watched his hill fort burn, Segotrix's anger became more and more palpable. Survivors were running through the woods in all directions.

Then, when it became clear that the Romans had found and fired the settlement, Segotrix lost control. Grasping Marcus by the hair he pulled his head back and raised his sword.

"Die, Roman!" he shouted.

Marcus knew this was the end. He was no longer afraid – he was beyond fear. Closing his eyes he waited.

"No, Segotrix! Stop!"

Marcus cautiously opened one eye. A Briton, even larger than Segotrix, had suddenly come upon them. With a scowl Segotrix lowered his sword but kept his hold on Marcus's hair.

"Why should I spare this Roman? He's a coward. He deserves to die."

"Caswallon wants him."

As Marcus waited to see what Segotrix would do he wondered who this Briton was that could order Segotrix about and how Caswallon, whoever he might be, knew about him.

Segotrix hesitated then reluctantly letting Marcus go and pushing him towards the Briton he snarled

"Take him, then."

As Marcus stumbled towards the Briton he wondered if his fate had only been deferred. He would not know until he came face to face with this Caswallon.

As he took his arm the Briton told him

"I am Comm. Caswallon is our High King and he has sent me to get you because he has heard that you are Caesar's son. We have many days travel before us. Come along, Segotrix."

Comm led the way through the woods followed by a scowling Segotrix to a track where they found several chariots waiting.

"You will come in my chariot, Roman" Comm ordered.

He helped Marcus into the first chariot and, scarcely waiting for Segotrix to climb into the next one in line, gave the order to move off.

Marcus was amazed by the skill of the charioteers as they moved swiftly through the light summer night. He found it difficult to make out the track but the Britons drove as swiftly as if it were broad daylight. When the track joined a wider road Comm stopped the column and sent one of the men back the way they had come to see if they were being pursued. While they waited they descended from the chariots and rested by the side of the track. Marcus took the opportunity to catch up on some sleep. Comm woke him some hours later.

"Come, Roman, we must get to the stronghold as soon as we can. The Romans are too busy making their encampment to bother with us tonight so we must make as much speed as possible."

Marcus clambered back up into the chariot. He felt elated and he now saw the way clear before him. Once he had the location of the stronghold and discovered its defences he would escape, find Caesar and lead him back to the stronghold. Caesar would be in his debt, and all Marcus's troubles would be over.

CHAPTER FOURTEEN

Comm pushed the men and only stopped to rest the horses. Marcus snatched his sleep when he could. The weather stayed fine and they made good progress. Marcus tried to find out where they were going but Comm, although he seemed friendly enough, always evaded the question.

One morning Marcus woke to find that Comm had taken one of the spare horses and gone. When he asked where Comm had gone he was told to "Mind your own business, Roman."

Marcus hoped Comm had not deserted him. The men had made it quite clear that they resented the presence of a Roman in their midst and only Comm's tight control over them had prevented Marcus from ill-treatment or worse.

To Marcus's relief Comm came into the camp late that evening and immediately called the men together.

"Caesar's ships have been damaged in a storm. He has withdrawn to the coast to make repairs. We will not travel tonight. Get some rest. We'll continue our journey tomorrow."

As the men dispersed one of them dug Marcus in the ribs, saying, "Don't they have proper seas where you come from, Roman?"

The men laughed. Marcus gave a sour smile, not bothering to reply.

The next day the chariots kept up a steady pace all day long. When the few people that they met along the track asked for news Comm always told them the same thing – the Romans had gone back to the coast but they must arm themselves for an attack at any time. They never stopped to hunt for food. One of the men would see a rabbit, pig or some other animal, tap his driver's shoulder to let him know his intention, jump off the chariot, seize and kill the animal, run after chariot and leap back on with his prize. The chariots never slackening their pace. If the man had to run fast to catch up with them he was urged on with shouts of encouragement. It reminded Marcus of the chariot races in Rome.

At the end of the day, when they were sitting round the fire after their evening meal, Comm often asked Marcus about his life in Rome. He seemed very interested in all Marcus had to tell him. He was particularly sympathetic when he heard how Marcus had been left behind the year before. He asked many questions and got Marcus to repeat his story several times. Once he asked him about his parentage and Marcus told him what he had told Segotrix.

"So Caesar is your father?"

"Yes, although he cannot acknowledge me, of course."

"No, I see that. He would have to keep it secret even from his closest associates." Comm agreed.

Marcus was relieved when Comm, appearing to have tired of the subject, turned the talk to other things.

The third day after leaving Segotrix's territory, the woods became dense and marshy, the sun glinting on the water on either side of the track, making their eyes ache. Soon the marsh turned to streams and the streams became a river which they followed for some miles. During the midday rest Comm warned Marcus, "We're nearly at the stronghold."

Marcus began to feel apprehensive. Seeing this Comm said, "Don't worry, Roman. Caswallon will not kill you out of hand I am sure, at least not yet. You are too useful as a hostage. He won't want to harm you."

At mid-afternoon they arrived at a wooden bridge over the river. Once across they found themselves in an extensive settlement at the foot of a large hill surrounded by enormous ramparts.

As he led the way through the crowds in the settlement Comm was greeted on all sides. Marcus saw many curious glances directed at himself. Upon reaching the ramparts Comm led them through the entrance and up the hill. This fort was much larger than Segotrix's and, by the time they reached the top, the horses were blowing hard. The chariots were driven into a large compound where hundreds of chariots were placed in orderly rows. Marcus had never seen so many. He found the sight depressing, remembering the havoc caused last year amongst the Roman infantry by the British chariots. Caesar would not find this fort as easily conquered as that of Segotrix.

Once inside the perimeter fence he stood regaining his breath and looking at the view, which was spectacular. Turning round to look on all sides he could see wooded hill upon wooded hill for miles. Bringing his gaze back to the fort the full extent of the defences were laid out before him, the staggered ramparts, the deep ditches and the wooden fence completely surrounding the whole plateau. The river far below glinting in the sun.

"Impressive, isn't it?" Comm remarked.

"The place is impregnable!" Marcus agreed.

Waving his hand at the view Comm told him.

"This stronghold is so well hidden that the Romans will never find it and the defences are so strong that it will never be taken – unless, of course, somebody knew their way here. And even if they did find it, once the bridge has been destroyed the only way across the river would be to wade – which would be difficult since the riverbed has sharpened stakes embedded in it."

Marcus realized that this was what he had been waiting for. Comm must be very confident of keeping him here if he felt he could explain the defences in such detail. Well, he would soon discover his mistake if Marcus had anything to do with it! If he could escape and lead Caesar to the stronghold think how grateful he would be! Once here he was sure Caesar would have some way of dealing with the defences – he was Caesar after all! He was excited at the prospect. Feeling himself being watched he turned to find Comm regarding him with a smile.

"I must leave you now, I have to see Caswallon. I can trust you not to try to escape? I assure you it would be useless."

"You have my word I will not try to escape."

"I'll not *try*, I *will!*" Marcus mentally added as he watched Comm stride away.

Thinking that the sooner he escaped the better before Comm returned, Marcus walked confidently towards the entrance. The place was crowded and nobody seemed to take any notice of him. All the men were intent on sharpening their weapons, and the women and children were busy piling up heaps of stones at regular intervals along the ramparts. Probably to be used with slingshots he thought. This gave him an idea. If he could go to Caesar not only with the whereabouts of the stronghold and its defences but also the number of fighting men, chariots, weapons and so on he could not fail to impress him. He decided to abandon his escape attempt temporarily and walk round the whole of the inside of the perimeter fence. Caesar would never be able to take this stronghold unless he had his, Marcus's, help. He continued his inspection. Clustered together in one section was a collection of huts one of which was probably Caswallon's so better to avoid them. There were dozens of grain pits, an enclosure containing a few tired looking cattle, another crammed with sheep. They would be able to sit out a siege for some time. He was only half way round when Comm caught up with him.

"There you are. I have just left Caswallon. He has decided that you can make yourself useful helping the physician in the hospital."

Being in the hospital would not be pleasant, there would be some gruesome sights and smells but escape could be easy if he planned things properly.

"I would be very glad to help in the hospital."

"I told Caswallon you would. Come along."

Marcus registered the fact that Comm seemed to be on intimate terms with Caswallon.

Comm led the way to a large hut situated near the rear of the fort and some distance from the other dwellings. Marcus braced himself to expect the worst but inside it was cool in spite of the central fire. There were no smells as the clean rushes on the floor gave out a pleasant odour. He was surprised to see everything looking so spotless. Only a few of the pallets ranged along both sides of the hut were occupied.

"Uxel!"

Comm called and a very small, muscular man appeared.

"Uxel, Caswallon has sent this Roman hostage to help you.You could be busy in the next few days."

Uxel looked Marcus up and down. He did not seem very impressed.

"Any experience in a hospital, Roman?" he asked.

"No" said Marcus, shortly.

"I'll leave you then."

Comm seemed anxious to be off.

"I may not see you again, Rutilius.Try to stay out of trouble and all could come out right for you."

Marcus was sorry to see him go. He had come to think of him almost as a friend.

Uxel gave him no time to ponder on his situation as he briskly outlined Marcus's duties. Nothing very gruesome Marcus was relieved to hear.

"Make sure the fire burns. Help me as required.You never touch a patient unless I am with you and you will always wash your hands before and after touching a patient, that is extremely important.You renew the rushes every day.You will leave the dirty rushes by the door and bring in and lay the fresh rushes you will find there.You will sleep on any pallet that is unoccupied.You will not leave the hut under any circumstances. If I have any suspicion that you are about to escape or if you attempt to harm any of my patients I'll tie you to a pallet.You will find life much easier if you co-operate. Do you understand?"

Marcus nodded. He would leave the hut as and when he wanted. Uxel was only half his size, he should be no problem when the time came.

As if he could read his mind Uxel growled

"And don't think about trying to overpower me, Roman. I am stronger than I look and I hate Romans. Now wash your hands.This man needs his foot dressed.You can hold him down."

As he worked under Uxel's directions Marcus decided that the best course of action would be to do everything the physician asked of him until he saw an opportunity to escape.

Late in the afternoon the wounded men began arriving and Marcus was kept busy assisting Uxel. Uxel's manner towards his patients was entirely different to the way he treated other people. He worked slowly and methodically, seeming not to hurry but no injured man went long without treatment. They both worked late into the night. When dawn came Marcus was asleep on his feet and Uxel ordered him to rest. He fell gratefully onto a pallet from which a dead man had just been removed and was asleep before his head touched the pillow.

It was late in the morning when he was woken by Uxel. The hospital was nearly full of wounded men. As he worked Uxel talked to the men, reassuring them and encouraging them to talk about how they got their wounds. From this Marcus learnt that Caesar's camp had been attacked and many Romans had been killed and wounded. Uxel did not even try to hide his delight at the news especially when it became clear that the consensus of opinion amongst the men was that one more battle and Caesar would be defeated.

Marcus felt very depressed. He found himself thinking the unthinkable – what happened to him if Caesar was defeated and killed? The probable answer was one he did not wish to contemplate.

By the next evening everything had changed. Uxel and Marcus were overwhelmed with wounded. Uxel even trusted Marcus to administer opium to any mortally wounded man. Putting together snatches of conversation it appeared that there had been a major battle. Caswallon had been badly defeated. The Britons were now as depressed as they had been elated the day before. Uxel hardly spoke as he worked them both hard without stopping for food or drink.

There were no spare pallets that night. Marcus slumped down with his back to the wall and was soon asleep despite the groans and cries of the wounded.

While he slept he dreamt he had a visitation from Jupiter who appeared in front of him. Jupiter spoke, "Wake, Marcus, wake!"

"Who is that?"

Marcus roused himself. It was no dream! Jupiter was still there. He tried to see him clearly but the god was enveloped in a cloak of some dark material the hood of which covered his head completely.

"A friend. Now is your chance to escape and find Caesar."

It must be Jupiter otherwise how would he know his name and also use the informal mode of address?

Jupiter beckoned

"Come quickly, follow me."

Marcus looked round for Uxel but he appeared to be engrossed in bandaging a man's hand. Surely he had heard? Uxel continued with his task.

"Come, Marcus, at once!" Jupiter said impatiently.

"I come, O Jupiter Optimus Maximus."

Marcus answered formally – the gods did not like mortals to be familiar.

As he followed the god he thought he heard a smothered laugh but he could have been mistaken.

Once outside the hut Marcus stopped to breathe in the night air but Jupiter would not allow him to pause and grasping his arm he urged him on. Marcus was surprised to find how human the god's hand felt.

"Come quickly," Jupiter urged.

Men and chariots were streaming through the entrance in their hundreds. More men were putting horses to chariots. At the same time men, women and children, some driving cattle before them, were trying to enter the fort. Cursing the people and cattle in their way the charioteers almost ran over them in their anxiety to leave.

"Why are they running away? Has Caesar come?"

Marcus was elated.

"The alliance between the tribes has broken down. The men are going home. Caswallon is on his own now."

Men carrying burning torches thrust their way past them.

"Run, Marcus!" Jupiter repeated, "Before they burn down the bridge. Go to Caesar!"

Marcus began to run. It was difficult going against the tide of people and animals coming in but by much pushing and shoving he got through at last. One of the charioteers, seeing him struggling, stopped his chariot and pulled him on board. The chariot rattled over the bridge just as the first torch was put to the timbers. When they reached the other side the charioteer reined in his horses. Looking back Marcus saw the settlement going up in flames. There was no sign of Jupiter.

"Did they kill that Roman hostage?" The man asked.

Giving Marcus no time to reply he continued, "I hope so but if I come across him I'll kill him – only good Roman is a dead one, that's what I say! I'll have to leave you here. I'm going home."

Thanking him Marcus climbed down. His feet had scarcely touched the ground when the man whipped up his horses and vanished into the crowd. Now he had to decide which way to go. While he stood, irresolute, a group of men approached. One stopped, peering at Marcus in the light of the flames from the burning settlement.

"Here's that Roman hostage!"

"It can't be. I heard that Caswallon killed him."

"Yes it is. I saw him when he came to the fort with Comm."

He stopped to scrutinise a petrified Marcus. His companions, who were by now some yards further on, called to him impatiently.

"Come on – we want to get home!"

With another searching look the man ran to catch up with them. Marcus saw him speaking urgently to them. They all stopped and looked back. Then, to Marcus's horror, they turned round and came back to where Marcus stood, surrounding him. Marcus was too terrified to move. They looked very large and very fierce and the light from the flames made sparks run up and down their drawn swords.

"He doesn't look like a Roman to me" one of them said scornfully.

Marcus tried to look small and insignificant.

"I tell you he is the hostage – I saw him come in with Comm." The man insisted. "He's escaped. He should be killed."

He raised his sword. One of the other men, who seemed to be the leader, pushed the sword down.

Addressing Marcus directly the first man asked, "Are you the Roman?"

"No, I am not. Have you seen Comm? I must have missed him in this crowd."

"Why do you want to find Comm?" the man sounded suspicious.

"We were going home together. We're related."

"Atrebatian are you?" the man enquired.

Marcus did not know if this was a good thing or not so took a chance.

"Of course."

"You don't sound Atrebatian to me."

One of the men opined. They took a step nearer.

"On my mother's side, of course" Marcus said hastily.

"I still think we should kill him."

"Oh! You *want* Comm to come and burn down all our huts and turn us all into slaves for killing one of his relatives do you?"

"How do you know he is one of Comm's relatives?"

"How do you know that he isn't?"

The two men began to wave their swords at each other. A fight looked imminent. There was a tense pause then one of the two men lowered his sword saying, "I'm going home"

He turned and began making his way down the track between the crowds. One by one the others followed until Marcus was left standing by the side of the track. Then he began to shake and feel cold and hot by turns. The sweat ran down his face in streams. He felt an overwhelming urge to get away from these people. He felt that everyone was watching him just waiting for a chance to kill him.

Calling on Jupiter Optimus Maximus for aid, he plunged into the dense forest bordering the track. A few paces in and it was completely dark. The forest was so dense that not even the light from the burning settlement could penetrate the gloom. Falling over tree roots and bruising himself on unseen trees he ran until he had to stop for breath. The only sounds rustlings from the trees and faint scrabblings of unknown creatures in the undergrowth. It was then that he realized he was lost and had no idea in which direction Caesar's camp lay.

CHAPTER FIFTEEN

Marcus knew that panic was not an ideal state when lost. Knowing this was one thing, acting on it was another. When he thought of the Barbarians who were after his blood he panicked. When he thought of his present situation – no food, no water, no idea where he was and only the clothes he stood up in, he panicked.

By dawn he found himself in a clearing and, without realizing what he was doing, he began to walk round and round talking to himself. He called on Jupiter for aid but Jupiter did not come. Then he called on all the gods, any god but there was no reply. Eventually he became so tired he lay down just where he was on the damp grass and immediately fell into a deep slumber.

The sun shining into the clearing woke him. He was very stiff and stood up with difficulty. Once he began to move about he felt better. A good night's sleep had made all the difference. He was thinking more rationally but, although he was extremely hungry, his main concern was finding water. This gave him a purpose and he began to look for a stream. He searched the clearing in the hope that he would not have to venture back into the forest but to his disappointment he found no sign of so much as a puddle. This was a grave setback but he felt confident he could work out which direction he should take.

He was certain that Caesar would take the track. No Commander would run the risk of being ambushed in a forest. Therefore his next move was to find the track. The trouble was he had no idea how far he had travelled the previous night. He did remember that the track ran alongside the river so, if he could find a stream he could both quench his thirst and follow the stream in order to reach the river and also the track. He would then follow the track towards the sea. Caesar would be coming from the sea so they must meet. Find a stream and all his problems would vanish.

The best way to achieve this was to listen for the sound of water which still left him with the problem of the direction he should take. He did not want to wander round in this forest for longer than necessary. Calling on Jupiter for aid as well as any other god that might be listening, he closed his eyes, spun round several times, stopped, opened his eyes, fixed his gaze on the first tree he saw and set off in that direction.

He made his way with difficulty through the forest climbing over fallen trees where he could and working his way round those he could not negotiate. He wished he had something with which to cut a path. His hands were soon sore and bleeding, his breeches mere strips of cloth. Once he came through the trees to a green, smooth open space. He would rest here. Just in time he saw the gleam of water and realized it was a swamp. He debated whether the water would be fit to drink and decided against it. He was bound to find a stream soon.

Animals ran away in panic at his approach. Once he came face to face with a huge wild boar. Its tusks were enormous. He froze. It stared at him for what seemed like several decades then turned and lumbered away. He paused frequently to listen for the sound of water until he thought he heard something other than the twitter of birds. He could not tell from which direction the sound came as the air had become very still and heavy. One by one the birds fell silent. It was difficult to breathe and he felt hot and sticky.

Then in the distance came the first rumble of thunder. He tried to speed up but the undergrowth was very dense. It became darker and darker, the thunder nearer. Flashes of lightning lit up the trees. Soon it began to rain, the enormous drops pattering on the leaves of the trees sounding like the Army striking their shields with their swords. The temperature dropped and he began to shiver. Eventually he came to a clearing containing large gorse bushes. Perhaps one would afford him some shelter. He searched until he found a bush large enough for him to crawl into. He was relieved to find that inside it was perfectly dry. He would stay here until the storm had passed. Peering out of his shelter at the rain which was now coming down in sheets, he cheered himself with the thought that the rain would swell the stream making it easier to locate.

The storm was now directly overhead. The lightning and the crashing thunder were simultaneous. Jupiter must be trying to tell him something through the lightning. Even as this thought came into his mind, he was thrown backwards as a tree on the other side of the clearing was struck by a bolt of lightning and exploded. Picking himself up he looked out and saw a tree with smoke rising from a split down the middle. Jupiter was sending him a message! As soon as the rain stopped he would take the tree as a marker and go in that direction.

He vowed that once he got back to Rome the first thing he would do would be to go to the Temple of Jupiter Optimus Maximus and sacrifice the most expensive pure white animal he could afford.

Once the storm had rumbled away he felt safe enough to leave the shelter of the bush. Using the still smoking tree as a guide he began to trek through the forest once more. He had not progressed very far when just ahead he heard the unmistakeable sound of running water. Pushing his way impatiently through the trees he came upon a stream in full spate. Water at last!

Thanking Jupiter he drank until he could drink no more then sat down on the bank to rest. Now that he was no longer thirsty his hunger took over. Perhaps he could catch a fish, it could not be that difficult. Scrambling down the bank he began searching the shallows. Sure enough a large fish was swimming slowly backwards and forwards. Kneeling down he tried to catch it but it swiftly darted away. He searched up and down the stream for some time but saw no more fish. Frustrated, he climbed back to the bank. There must be something he could eat. He had seen Comm's men catch food often enough on the journey to the stronghold. As he stood, idly prodding a bush with his foot, he disturbed a small animal which he recognized as a dormouse.

The last time he had tasted this luxury had been at Baeae when it had been served sprinkled with honey and poppy seed but he would be quite happy to eat it plain. He forced himself to stand still until the dormouse was nearly up to his feet then pounced, catching it by its fluffy tail. Now he had to kill it. He was considering the best way to do this and had decided that banging its head against a tree would be the easiest method, when it swung its body round and bit him. Cursing, he dropped it then chased it until it fled down the bank and into a hole.

His hand was bleeding profusely and he remembered Uxel's insistence on wounds being thoroughly washed. He did not understand why but thought it best to do so. Although the wound was not deep it was painful. He held his hand in the stream until the pain gradually subsided and the bleeding had diminished. After wrapping it in a piece of cloth torn from his tunic he continued to follow the stream which proved to be more difficult than he had thought as it wandered about, sometimes almost disappearing then he had to find it again. Sometimes the trees stretched right down to the water's edge. On these occasions, afraid he would lose sight of the stream once he went into the trees, he got down into the water and waded until he was able to get back on the bank again.

He was getting tired and had to pause frequently. During one rest period he noticed some berries. Eagerly picking them he crammed them into his mouth washing them down with copious draughts of water. They were very bitter but it was the first food he had had in days. Almost immediately he vomited, violently. Exhausted, he realized he could go no further that day. He found a tree which overhung the stream and climbing up to a fork settled down to sleep.

For several days he followed the stream in this way, sleeping in a tree at night. At last, when the stream began to flow faster and become wider he knew he must be somewhere near the river. The thought of finding the track and people was the only thing that kept him going. He had tried to catch various animals, even birds but they easily eluded him and his experience with the berries left him very reluctant to try further experiments.

He was surprised to find that the lack of human contact was an even worse trial than the hunger. He had never in his life been completely alone before and even Murdia would have been welcome company. He vowed that once back in Rome he would never go anywhere near the country again.

He was becoming weaker and had to stop and rest more frequently. One night he did not have the strength to get into a tree so slept at the foot. The next day he could not bring himself to go on. He would just rest for the day. The next day he would continue to follow this stream for some reason which he could not remember but knew that it was important.

He lay at the foot of the tree with no idea of how much time had passed. Small creatures ran over his body but he made no attempt to catch them. A brown, cat-sized animal came and looked at him then turned away. He watched rabbits grazing within yards of his feet. If he only had the strength he could catch a feast. Perhaps tomorrow. Several times he crawled to the stream and drank but even that became too much trouble. He had a lucid moment during the night when he knew that he would probably die. He felt bitter – if only he had found Caesar he could have risen to an important position. Now there would be no funeral procession out of the city, no rites, no oration. His bones would lie in this dreadful forest until they turned to dust. Nobody would know what had become of him.

Both Jupiter and the Sibyl had played a nasty trick on him, the one almost saving him then leaving him to die, the other giving him false promises. He thought of Simplicia and hoped she had been able to get back to her tribe. Then his thoughts turned to his mother. He supposed he would see her soon in the Underworld. How would she greet him? As he drifted in and out of consciousness he thought he heard voices. He tried to call out but could not. If he could only attract attention – he did not care who found him, Roman or Barbarian, so long as he was found. With a great effort he picked up a piece of wood and banged it against the tree keeping up a regular rhythm. The voices came nearer and he managed a feeble croak. Into his field of vision came a pair of feet wearing regulation army sandals.

"It's another Barbarian, Gaius, kill him and let's get on with this foraging."

"No, wait – I think I know that face. It's Rutilius, we shared a tent once. He's in a bad way!"

"Are you sure? If we take back a Barbarian instead of meat you can explain to the Centurion!"

Gaius bent down and peered at Marcus who managed a feeble groan.

"It is you, isn't it?"

With an effort Marcus managed to nod.

"What has happened to you? Where did you get to when we left? Caesius Scaeva and I searched everywhere for you. Decrius was annoyed and Caesar was not too pleased. We thought we were going to be decimated. Help me to lift him Licinius."

As they began to lift him Marcus thanked Jupiter that he would not now die in this accursed forest.

Marcus spent the next few days in the hospital in Caesar's camp the Medicus keeping him in bed until he had built up his strength. Gaius often came to visit him and told him that Centurion Decrius Marcellinus had distinguished himself in battle and gained the Corona Civica.

"The what?" Marcus asked, puzzled.

"The Corona Civica. Its a crown made of oak leaves. You get it when you save the life of another soldier. Oh, and Caesius Scaeva was badly wounded. He's been sent back to the continent. You were very lucky we found you. Every time we went into the forest to hunt for food the Barbarians ambushed us. In the end Caesar gave orders that we were not to go too far from the track. Fortunately for you you were close by the track otherwise you would still be there – probably dead." He added, cheerfully.

"Thank you."

"That's alright. Wish you had been a soldier though, then I could have had the Corona Civica. Still, I am pleased we found you. Now I must go. My Centurion gave me special leave to see you but said I must get back by the seventh hour for sentry duty."

Once he was strong enough the Medicus, a Greek called Diaulus, ordered him to help load the wounded onto the carts as the hospital moved with the army.

"It will enable you to be entitled to food, otherwise you would have to find your own. Do you have any experience of medical work?"

Marcus enumerated the duties he had performed under Uxel's direction. After several searching questions, Diaulus said, "You seem to know how to help with dressing wounds. You will be very useful to me as most of my orderlies have some sort of fever brought on by this accursed weather."

As the days went by Diaulus gave Marcus more and more responsibility. But he was not so busy that he had forgotten his mission and had several times asked to see Caesar but Diaulus did not seem to understand the importance of Marcus's information.

"I must see Caesar. I know where the stronghold is." Marcus insisted.

"That is where we are going now, Rutilius."

"How did Caesar know where it was?"

Marcus was indignant. All that suffering for nothing!

"Somebody told him I expect – probably a prisoner."

Marcus felt very put out for several days. What would he do now? Why had Caesar not sent for him? Did Caesar even know that he was here?

Marcus was impatient to see Gaius and as soon as he saw him asked

"Does Caesar know I am here?"

"Oh yes, he has been told." Gaius looked guilty then blurted out.

"My Centurion told me he had orders from Caesar to find out where you had been all this time and if you had any useful information. I would have come to see you anyway." he added, hastily.

"Of course." Marcus did not bother to hide his sarcasm.

"Anyway, you don't know anything important as I told the Centurion."

"Anything I know I tell Caesar and only Caesar." Marcus said, stiffly.

"Right – I'll tell my Centurion then."

After an awkward silence of some minutes Gaius left.

Marcus fumed for the rest of the day. All he had gone through, all he had endured and for what?

His self-absorption was penetrated by a stir which went through the tent. Those men who were not wounded sat up straighter. The Medicus stopped what he was doing, the buzz of conversation died down. Caesar came into the tent alone. Nodding to the Medicus he made his way down the line of men stopping to speak to each one. Marcus continued to bind a head wound. Caesar waited until he had finished. When Marcus straightened up he looked into the eyes of Caesar. Caesar gazed back and smiled.

"Rutilius – you are better I see. Come outside with me."

Followed by dozens of pairs of curious eyes they left the tent.

Caesar waved away the aides who waited outside and, once they were at a safe distance stopped and faced Marcus.

"You were with the Barbarians a long time. You must have seen many things. I understand you know where the Barbarian Chief is. A – person – has already told me but I do need confirmation from a reliable source."

He waited, expectantly.

Nearly bursting with pride Marcus told Caesar everything he knew. Defences, weapons, number of chariots, men, stakes in the river, everything. Caesar listened in silence then said.

"This not only confirms what I have been told but you have given me some additional information. You have done well. When I have more time we must talk. I would like to know something of your history but that must wait. In the meantime stay with Diaulus he is very pleased with your help and seems to think you would make an excellent physician but I think we can do better than that. Now I must leave you."

"Thank you, Caesar," Marcus managed to stammer.

Caesar nodded and walked back to where his aides stood at a discreet distance.

Marcus wondered what Caesar had in mind for him. Did he want him to join the army? He had mixed feelings about that but he knew that if that was what Caesar wanted him to do he would do it.

CHAPTER SIXTEEN

As Marcus walked back into the hospital tent he knew that all eyes were upon him. One man could not contain himself.

"What did Caesar say to you, Rutilius?"

Everyone waited, even Diaulus paused in his work.

"It was private." Marcus told them.

"It must have been pretty important – I mean – Caesar!" the men nodded in agreement.

Marcus could feel himself getting taller by the minute.

"I can't say," he said, importantly. "I am sworn to secrecy," he added for good measure.

"We understand. Leave him alone you men. If he can't say, he can't say."

All returned to their occupations except the first man who was not to be intimidated and was determined to have the last word.

"That's fine Rutilius, we all know who you look like!"

The men laughed

"That's enough," Diaulus said, firmly. The man grinned but said no more.

Diaulus spoke quietly to Marcus. "Is everything alright?"

Marcus nodded and went back to work. He was thankful for Diaulus's intervention. He knew there was much speculation among the men regarding his parentage. He suspected that there were even bets on it. He did not blame them, after all, once they were on the mend they had nothing to do all day except gossip.

They were very near the stronghold now. One morning, as Marcus climbed down from the hospital wagon after helping the last man on board, he felt a tap on his shoulder, when he turned he was astonished to see Segotrix.

"Greetings, Roman. I'm glad you're still alive."

"Are you a captive?" Marcus asked.

Segotrix laughed.

"Of course not. The four of us could see that Caswallon did not stand a chance so, to protect our people, we decided to throw in our lot with Caesar."

Marcus would have liked to know more about this apparent about-face but the column began to move off, the escorting soldiers had fallen in either side of the baggage train, the wagon in front started to move and Marcus jumped onto the hospital wagon. He was not going to get left behind again!

As the column moved through the forest toward the stronghold and attacks became more frequent Marcus was thankful for the soldier escort, some of whom ended up in the hospital wagon before the day was out. It was not a comfortable journey. The foraging parties had fired the settlements after taking as much food as they could and the air was full of smoke behind them but now the air in front was also thick with smoke as Caswallon had obviously ordered his people to fire their fields. The foraging parties reported that all the cattle had gone. As he choked on the acrid smoke Marcus's mind ran continuously on food. He relived every banquet he had ever attended. Food supplies became short as the foraging parties were attacked as soon as they left the safety of the column. The Britons kept pace with them in the woods either side of the track from which they swiftly despatched careless or unwary soldiers. Marcus did not ask what was in the thin stew which was distributed at the end of the day's march.

When they arrived at the foot of the escarpment the hospital tent was, as usual, sited as close to the fighting as possible. In pauses from his duties Marcus was able to watch the opening stages of the attack on the stronghold but once the wounded began to come in he had no time to admire the efficiency of the Roman Army. All four orderlies having now recovered sufficiently to be on duty Marcus's responsibilities were reduced to handing forceps, scalpels and probes to Diaulus as required and generally making himself useful. The cries of the wounded as Diaulus dug out stones and other missiles embedded in their bodies was now such a familiar part of his world that he no longer heard them.

During the afternoon Decrius Marcelinus was brought in with multiple wounds. Marcus was glad that Decrius was unconscious as Diaulus probed deeply into the Centurion's body. When Diaulus indicated that he was finished Marcus asked him what were Decrius's chances of survival. Diaulus shook his head. Marcus was grieved. He remembered the Centurion's rough kindness. All he could do was to make him as comfortable as possible. Decrius died in the early hours of the morning without regaining consciousness.

By the end of the day the settlement had been taken. Funeral rites were observed for the men killed in action and Diaulus gave Marcus permission to attend Decrius's funeral.

Once he had attended the funeral rites Marcus felt he had done all he could to ensure Decrius' smooth passage to the Underworld.

As the stronghold was full of cattle and sheep Caesar ordered them to be slaughtered to provide the men with a much needed feast. Marcus, and the men who were fit enough to walk, went to the feast which continued late into the night. Some wine had been procured and Marcus indulged himself. He felt that he deserved it. At the height of the feast Marcus looked for Segotrix but could not find him.

The men were encouraged to relax and only perform necessary tasks. Everyone carried out the order with enthusiasm. Marcus, fuelled by food and good wine, decided that the time had come for Caesar to be made aware of who he was. He went to Caesar's tent where he found Titus Atticus Labienus, Caesar's Second in Command busily writing. There was no sign of Caesar. Marcus rather tipsily demanded to know where Caesar was but receiving only an expressionless stare in response beat a hasty retreat. The feasting went on for three days at the end of which even Marcus had had enough.

Suddenly Caesar appeared in the camp without anyone being aware of how he got there. Now, Marcus thought, now I will be sent for but no summons came. The only patients in the hospital were a few men still recovering from their wounds and the usual injuries sustained in the normal work of the camp. The four orderlies were hard put to it to keep busy and Marcus found himself redundant for the first time in a month. He spent a great deal of his time sitting outside the tent in the sun which is where Comm found him.

"Hello, Rutilius, taking it easy as usual I see!"

Marcus was pleased to see his friend was still alive.

"What are you doing here?"

"Caswallon has asked me to negotiate peace terms. Segotrix is dead" he added.

"How?"

"He and his brothers attacked Caesar's beachhead. They were badly defeated. It made Caswallon realize that he could not overcome the most efficient Army in the world."

"I thought Segotrix had decided to support Caesar?"

"Segotrix was only interested in improving his status. He was told about the plan to attack the beachhead and took a gamble which he lost."

This prompted Marcus to ask a question which had been bothering him for some time.

"Whose side are *you* on? Roman or Celt?"

Comm answered with a question of his own.

"Had any more visits from Jupiter lately?"

He laughed at Marcus's look of astonishment.

"It was *you!*"

"Was it? To more serious business. During a break in the negotiations – they are interminable by-the-way, Caesar is getting impatient – Caesar spoke of you."

"Of *me?*" Marcus was half excited, half afraid.

"He is going to offer you a post on his staff. A very special post. I would advise you to take it. I think – we both think – that you would be admirably suited to the work."

"What is it?"

"I can't tell you, that must come from Caesar himself but you would be a fool to refuse. What I can tell you is that it is something you will enjoy. I am warning you about this so that you can think it over but remember, Caesar is taking it for granted that you will accept the post. Asking you is just a formality so far as he is concerned and it would be extremely foolish to refuse."

"Thank you, Comm. You have been a good friend to me."

"I hope we can work together in the future." Comm said, enigmatically. "Now I must get back – as I said Caesar is an impatient man!"

Marcus found time hanging heavy on his hands. Once again he felt that he did not fit in – he was neither in the Army nor a civilian. He had already decided that, whatever the post was that Caesar was offering, he would take it. Once he was on Caesar's staff he could expect people to treat him with deference – probably even Titus Atticus Labienus!

To relieve his boredom he took to walking round the camp at odd moments of the day and night. On one of these perambulations he saw dozens of men, women and children being brought into the camp. Seeing a soldier digging out a ditch he asked him who they were. The soldier was only too pleased for an excuse to rest.

"Hostages, I expect. Caesar likes to have plenty of hostages."

"Will they be killed?" Marcus asked.

"Only the old or sick – they'll be sent to the arena. The rest will be sold, not a bad life so long as they get a good master. Won't see Britain again, of course. Caesar will make quite a few sesterces on that lot I shouldn't wonder. I wouldn't mind…"

"You, soldier! Stop chattering like an old woman at the market and dig!"

The red-faced Centurion who had appeared as if from nowhere, hit the soldier across the shoulders with his vine staff. Muttering, but not too loudly, the soldier got on with his task. The Centurion turned and glared at Marcus who thought it best to stroll casually away idly following the hostages as they were led to Caesar's tent and lined up. As he looked along the line of dispirited Britons his attention was caught by one of the men. Through the dirt he thought he recognized

Anamnus. He walked towards him only to be stopped by one of the soldiers guarding them.

"Halt! Nobody is to speak to the hostages."

Anamnus raised his head and looked at Marcus. He showed no sign of recognition. His face was without expression, his eyes empty. Marcus smiled at him but he only lowered his head, dejectedly.

Marcus remembered the talks they had had round the fire, the way Anamnus had nursed him when he was ill, his concern when he became depressed. He wished there was something he could do for him, he could not bear the thought of Anamnus being sold to someone like Annia. He turned this over in his mind for sometime and then it came to him – he would buy him!

He did not stop to think where the money would come from but went straight to the soldier who had turned him away and asked him how he could buy one of the hostages. The soldier referred him to his Centurion who said it was impossible – he would have to wait until they reached Rome and bid for the hostage at the slave auction. This did not suit Marcus at all. He decided to go direct to Caesar – he must have finished the negotiations otherwise there would be no hostages.

He was stopped at the entrance to Caesar's tent by an armed guard. A heated discussion between Marcus and the guard brought Labienus out to see what all the noise was about. Once again Marcus asked to see Caesar and once again he was refused. He raised his voice, Labienus began to threaten, the guard drew his sword and Caesar, wearing a thunderous frown, appeared from the depths of the tent.

"Stop all this noise at once!" he roared.

Silence. To the guard: "Sheath your sword."

To Labienus: "Let him come in."

To Marcus: "I can spare you very little time."

Without waiting to see if he followed Caesar turned and entered the tent. Once inside Caesar sat down and waved his hand at a table covered with scrolls.

"You can see how busy I am. I hope it is important."

Marcus explained how Anamnus had saved his life when he was ill, how indebted to him he was. He stopped when he saw Caesar beginning to drum his fingers impatiently on the table.

"I am going to give you a job on my staff, Rutilius. I have no time now to explain it to you. I assume you will take it?"

Marcus nodded.

"Good. You will need somebody you can trust and who better than a slave you have saved from an uncertain future? Do you have enough money to buy him?"

Marcus flushed and stammered.

For the first time Caesar smiled.

"No matter, I will give him to you as part of your salary."

He scribbled on a scrap torn from a scroll.

"Take this to Labienus. He will sort it out for you. Now you must leave me to read these reports."

As Marcus began to stammer his profound thanks Caesar waved him away and, picking up a scroll, began to read.

Labienus was not pleased with Caesar's orders but reluctantly carried them out. Anamnus was brought to Caesar's tent. He looked surprised when he found he was not to be killed on the spot. Marcus explained to him that he was now his slave. It was clear that Anamnus was torn between gratitude and profound humiliation.

As Marcus left Caesar's tent with Anamnus walking respectfully behind him, he reflected that he was now a slave owner, the holder of an important position on Caesar's staff and the recipient of an unknown quantity of denarii each month.

CHAPTER SEVENTEEN

The march back to the beachhead camp was slow. There were large numbers of hostages, also many cattle. At least they had decent food for which Marcus was thankful. He spent the time instructing Anamnus in his duties. Since Marcus was no longer part of the hospital staff he had to walk. Anamnus appeared to be extremely depressed and would not speak, he also refused to eat. Marcus was afraid that part of his wages were about to die on him. He had no intention of letting that happen. He began to talk to Anamnus about his new life but got no reaction, Anamnus just plodded on, his eyes never leaving his feet. The nearer they got to the sea the more despondent Anamnus became. Marcus would like to have asked Comm for his advice but Comm was with Caesar most of the time then, one evening, as Marcus was watching Anamnus prepare his food and wondering how he could induce him to share it, Comm came and sat by his side and Marcus took the opportunity to ask

"Can you give me some advice?"

"What about?"

"It's my slave. Caesar gave him to me as part of my salary."

"Has Caesar spoken to you yet?"

"No."

"Don't worry, he will. What is wrong with your slave? Anamnus, isn't it?"

Marcus wondered if there was anything Comm did not know.

"We were quite friendly when I was with the Barbarians but now he won't speak or eat."

"He is a Briton, Rutilius, he probably feels upset at leaving the Island. He knows he will never come back. Besides he does not know what to expect. For all he knows you will sell him when you get to Rome – you are perfectly entitled to – he belongs to you. You might feel you do not want the responsibility."

Suddenly Stronnius came to Marcus's mind. He remembered how despondent he had been when he thought Sextus might not free him after all.

"I don't want to sell him, I like him, in fact I was thinking of manumitting him sometime in the future."

"Have you told *him* that?"

"No, I've only just thought of it."

"You should let the man know where he stands. It might make all the difference. On the other hand if he has made up his mind to die there is nothing you can do that will prevent him."

After thinking over what Comm had said Marcus decided to take his advice and walked over to where Anamnus was listlessly arranging Marcus's bed under one of the wagons.

"Leave that, Anamnus. Sit down here with me."

He indicated a fallen tree trunk well away from the bustle of the camp.

"What happened to your mother?"

At first Marcus thought he was going to ignore him then Anamnus burst into furious speech.

"You Romans killed her. You kill everything you touch! Now you can kill me! I am no man's slave, least of all a Roman's. Take your sword. Send me to the Otherworld."

As he said this Anamnus leapt to his feet. Marcus too jumped up, in fright.

"You know I have no sword, Anamnus, and even if I had I could not kill you, you are my friend."

"How can I be your friend? You own me. Is a cauldron a friend, or a sandal?"

"Sit down, Anamnus, and listen to me if, after you have listened, you still want to go to the Otherworld I will borrow that soldier's sword and kill you. Now will you listen?"

Marcus was elated when Anamnus nodded.

"There is nothing I can do to make you a freeman until we get to Rome. Once we are there I will make sure you get your manumission. I'm really sorry about your mother. I didn't kill her, you know. There is nothing for you here. Segotrix is dead, your settlement burnt. Would it not be sensible for you to come to Rome with me, be made a freeman and perhaps make enough money so that you can come back to Britain and start a new life?"

Anamnus was silent for a long time.

"Why should I believe you? You are a Roman."

Anamnus walked back to the wagon and carried on making Marcus's bed.

At least he has spoken to me and didn't take up my offer to kill him so I have made some progress, Marcus thought.

He wished there was some way he could prove to Anamnus that he was genuinely trying to help him. As if sent by the gods an unexpected opportunity came his way. When the hostages were given their evening meal a fight broke out apparently over the distribution. The soldiers watched in amusement for a time but when it became clear that things were getting out of hand and people were getting hurt they moved in to break up the fighting only to be set upon themselves. Order was only restored after a complete cohort had gone in with drawn swords and rescued their comrades.

Soon after he had gone to sleep Marcus was woken by the sound of voices. He wished they would let him sleep. When he recognized Anamnus's voice he became worried in case he was trying to get himself killed by baiting one of the sentries. The soldiers were very tense after the injuries inflicted in the fighting. Marcus made his way swiftly in the direction of the voices. In the dark he fell over something which yelped.

"Who is it?" he asked.

He felt a hand on his arm and Anamnus growled, "If you really want to show your remorse for the killing your countrymen have done, help me."

Marcus knew he had only to raise his voice to bring the sentries running. Instead he said, quietly, "I am not going to help you to get killed, Anamnus, so it is no good asking me."

"I shall have to trust you, I suppose." Anamnus sounded reluctant.

"The fight was started deliberately to cause a diversion and five hostages managed to escape. Nobody knows they have gone. We made sure of that. They are hidden with the horses and I have to get them out over the ramparts."

"With the horses! They'll be trampled to death!"

"You forget we are experts with horses."

Marcus considered. If he was discovered helping hostages to escape he had no doubt he would be on the receiving end of Caesar's considerable anger. Was it worth the risk of throwing everything away just to allow some Barbarians to escape slavery? He was conscious that Anamnus was watching him waiting for his decision. Sending a silent prayer to the Di Conservatores to preserve him Marcus asked

"How can I help?"

"We have to get them from the horse lines to the rampart and over it. Only the fittest men were chosen to escape so the rampart will be no problem. Once in the woods they will be safe."

Anamnus stopped, waiting for Marcus's brilliant solution. Marcus only wished he had one. The problem was that the 200 foot gap between the horse lines and the rampart was used as a thoroughfare day and night. He thought for a moment and then an idea slowly began to form. When he had worked it out he turned to Anamnus.

"Are these men about your height and build?"

"Roughly, yes." Anamnus sounded puzzled.

"You and I are going to go for a walk as we cannot sleep."

"I thought you were going to help us. I should have known that you..."

"Do listen. Each man will take your place one after the other. Nobody looks at slaves anyway. As soon as I indicate that it is safe he will climb over the ramparts – that will be the most dangerous part –

then I will come back. The next one can join me and so on until they have all escaped. You must send them out when you see me opposite their hiding place. You must tell them to walk just behind me – they are supposed to be my slave."

"I don't think they will take kindly to being thought to be a Roman slave. They're warriors."

"Now look here, Anamnus. You asked me to help you. I am trying to do so. If I am caught I will be killed, even Caesar will not be able to save me. If I can take that risk they can put up with being thought to be slaves for a few minutes. Of course they can always stay here and be discovered when the servants come to get the horses in the morning."

Anamnus nodded and darted away. Marcus waited on tenterhooks until he returned to say that the men had agreed to follow the plan. As he began to make his way to the horse lines Marcus stopped him.

"Just one more thing. If you want to go with them I'll not stop you."

"I did think of it but then I remembered what you said. I can do more good by going to Rome. Once I am a freeman I can come back and lead my people against the Romans."

Marcus noticed he said "the Romans" and not "you Romans" so he presumed he had been forgiven.

"Besides," Anamnus continued, "you need somebody to look after you."

Four of the men had made their escape over the ramparts without incident. Only one more to go and it was getting light. Marcus strolled back past the picket lines. Anamnus despatched the last man who took his station just behind Marcus. Marcus was just about to wave the man over the ramparts when, in the early dawn light, he saw a figure coming towards him.

"So, Anamnus," he said loudly, hoping the Briton would realize the danger, "you must remember in future that I like my tunics kept clean."

The figure came nearer. Marcus's heart jumped as he recognized the tall figure of Caesar.

"Rutilius, up early I see." Caesar remarked, glancing at the man behind Marcus.

Marcus prayed the man would not panic and make a break for the rampart. Caesar obviously intended to stop and chat.

"Once we get to the main camp I will send someone for you. I think it is time we discussed your role on my staff."

"Yes, Caesar, thank you, Caesar," Marcus stammered.

Caesar nodded and went on his way. As soon as he had rounded the corner Marcus urged the man over the rampart. Once he had gone Marcus breathed a sigh of relief and went back to where Anamnus waited.

"Thank you, you will be remembered for this by our bards who will sing your praises to the people."

Marcus was not quite sure how he should respond but fortunately Anamnus did not seem to expect a reply.

They reached the beachhead camp that day. Having had very little sleep the night before Marcus was pleased to stagger into the first unoccupied tent he came to. He was woken by Anamnus who told him a messenger had come for him from Caesar. As he helped Marcus into a clean tunic he wished him luck.

Caesar seemed to be in a good mood. Marcus had been mortally afraid that, somehow, his part in the escape of the hostages had been discovered.

"There you are, Rutilius. Sit down. Tell me something about yourself. How old are you?"

"About eighteen – I think."

"And who were your parents?"

"My mother was an ex-Vestal Virgin. She met a Tribune soon after she left the Order. I was the result."

Caesar became very still.

"A Vestal Virgin! What was her name."

"Julia."

Caesar's expression did not alter at the name. His cold, piercing eyes were fixed on Marcus's face.

"What was the name of this Tribune?"

"I don't know. I begged my mother to tell me but she refused. Perhaps she never knew it."

"Perhaps not. It could be extremely awkward for both of them if it ever came to light so it is best not to pursue the matter. I am sure you agree?"

As Marcus nodded he realized that Caesar would never acknowledge him as his son, even in private. However, it was enough to know that Caesar knew who he was.

Caesar became brisk.

"To business. I am sure you have been wondering what your duties will be. First the salary."

Caesar named a sum which made Marcus's head spin. He would never again have to worry about where his next meal was coming from or his debts in Rome and he could live in total comfort to the end of his days. The Sybil's prediction was coming true!

Caesar noted his reaction.

"I see that is satisfactory. As I intend to return next year and conquer the entire island your knowledge of the language, customs and the terrain will be invaluable to me. It has also been brought to my attention that we are somewhat alike. You could be taken for me – at a distance. This will be useful as there are times when I need to be in two places at the same time. I intend to go far, Rutilius."

Caesar paused, obviously awaiting some comment. Marcus pulled himself together.

"I should be honoured to serve you in any way I can, Gaius Julius Caesar," he replied, formally.

"Good. See my secretary. I have given him instructions that you are to be accommodated close to my tent. I want you available at all times from now on."

The weather became stormy and the ships which Caesar had sent for from the continent not arriving, Marcus was pleased when Caesar finally lost patience and embarked everyone on such ships as he had. It was extremely cramped but as the weather had abated somewhat Marcus was not unduly uncomfortable.

Everyone was in high spirits – they were going home to women, sun, warmth, baths, games, Rome.

Marcus stood with the rest of Caesar's staff and watched the Island recede into the distance. At long last he was on his way home!

Caesar noticed his excitement.

"You are on your way, Rutilius. Home, to a new life and who knows what adventures!"

Taking Marcus's arm and drawing him forward into the circle Caesar said, "Gentlemen, Rutilius here will be my second self. Any boring meetings or public occasions and I can send him. Unless of course it is a triumph!"

Everyone laughed.

"Just think, Caesar," one of the Tribunes said, "If your life is under threat all you have to do is send for Rutilius!"

Marcus joined in the general laughter. He felt wonderful. The Sibyl's prediction that he would one day become a great man of Rome was coming true! He was accepted by these men as one of themselves, he had a great life ahead of him. As for being killed in Caesar's stead – who could possibly want to harm Gaius Julius Caesar!